Bonnie Chronicles Compilation

Compilation

EROTIC LESBIAN ROMANCE

MIRANDA MARS

WARNING

This book contains sexually explicit scenes and adult language. It may be considered offensive to some readers. This book is for sale to adults ONLY.

* * * * * * * * * * * * * * * * * * *

Please store your files wisely where they cannot be accessed by underage readers.

Please feel free to send me an email. Just know that these emails are filtered by my publisher. Good news is always welcome.

Miranda Mars- **miranda_mars@awesomeauthors.org**

You might also want to check my blog for Updates and interesting info. http://miranda-mars.awesomeauthors.org/

About the Publisher

4Fun Publishing, a member of **BLVNP Incorporated**, 340 S. Lemon #6200, Walnut CA 91789, info@blvnp.com / legal@blvnp.com
NOTE: Due to the highly emotional reaction of some people to works of erotic fiction, any email sent to the above address that contains foul language or religious references is automatically deleted by our anti-spam software and will not be seen. All other communications are welcome.

DISCLAIMER

BONNIE CHRONICLES
Compilation

Erotic Lesbian Romance

By: Miranda Mars

© **Miranda Mars 2014**
ISBN: 978-1-62761-929-5

TABLE OF CONTENTS

Miranda Mars

SANDWICH SHOP
Seduction

Bonnie Chronicles 1

EROTIC LESBIAN ROMANCE

They are just everywhere, aren't they, Laura thought ruefully as she noticed the darling new black girl with short hair and a hall-of-fame bottom who was working the counter at lunch time these days at the little sandwich shop in the trendy alley behind her office building. The girl could be anything from eighteen to twenty-five; it was hard for Laura to judge. But she was completely lovely in a fresh, normal, not spectacularly beautiful, girl-next-door way. Dark, but not pitch black dark, with a charming smile, black hair that fell to her neck in back and around her ears at the sides, even white teeth, a slender but not negligible figure, and of course an ass that Laura could barely keep her eyes away from.

Oh god, she thought, I have fallen in love with a few asses before, and it just turns me to jelly every time. She thought, a trifle guiltily, of Makeeda's ass (her lesbian wife's) which was definitely one of them; a hall of famer if ever there was one. In fact, this girl—the little nameplate pinned to her blue golf shirt said 'Bonnie'—had an ass shaped very much like Makeeda's: not a hard, high, compact bubble ass but a fuller version, still a beautiful bubble ass but a swelling, curved, opulent, though not at all blubbery, rump. You wanted to dig your fingers into its resilience. Laura, hopelessly oral, wanted to kiss each round black moon for an eternity.

But she felt a little ashamed for being so horny for Bonnie after she got to know her a little, because the girl was completely guileless and friendly to a fault, almost perky, cute, unaware of her physical charms, but also perfectly certain that hers was no movie star quality beauty just waiting to be discovered. She was a normal, average, healthy, friendly girl. Unfortunately it's the type that sent Laura quickly around the bend.

She would deposit the change for Laura's sandwich back in Laura's palm and let her fingertips rest there for a moment before moving on to her next customer, as if this were a special, almost an intimate moment she was savoring. Laura certainly savored it, until she saw Bonnie do the same thing with several other customers, male and female, and realized it meant nothing. It was merely a friendly little gesture she was completely unaware of, though it spoke volumes about her sweet, simple nature.

Nevertheless, Laura tried not to dwell on Bonnie. There was no hope in that direction, she knew. Nevertheless, one afternoon after a weary spell of aimless meetings that had driven her nearly mad with boredom, she decided to go downstairs and out to the little alley where the sandwich shop was and flirt with Bonnie, as a way of getting everything at least briefly off her mind.

This in itself had little prospect of success since she and Bonnie had never exchanged more than two words, and Laura's radar told her in no uncertain terms that the girl was about as straight as she could be. Still, it was a change of pace, and she needed one.

It was close to three thirty in the afternoon, and so lunch was long over. This was coffee break time, and a few idle couples and solitary newspaper readers were lingering at the tables, preventing the sandwich shop staff from sweeping and closing, as they were clearly eager to do. Bonnie poured Laura a cup of coffee and took her money. She seemed a little wearier now than she usually appeared to Laura in the bustle and mild chaos of the lunch hour.

"I'll bet you're eager to close," Laura smiled to her, nodding casually at the other customers.

Bonnie smiled back, a wan, weary, but very friendly smile. "I get tired by this time of day," she confessed. "Can't help it. My feet get sore."

"I can imagine," Laura sympathized.

"You work around here? Haven't I seen you at lunch?"

Have you ever, darling, Laura thought. I come here every day since I saw that you work here. "That one," Laura pointed. "The big brown ugly one. Thirty-fourth floor."

She was looking too intently, she feared, at Bonnie's perfect black neck, and her earlobes where they were visible under her fringe of short black hair, and her sparkling even teeth, and her shiny black eyes, and her red fingernails, and her shapely forearms, and the way her small breasts pushed out against her blue golf shirt, evidently the 'uniform' of the sandwich shop since the other two employees were wearing that shirt too. I must stop scrutinizing her this way, Laura cautioned herself. I look like a predator, for goodness sake.

"Why don't you take a minute off and have a cup of coffee with me?" Laura asked, trying to make this request sound as casual as possible, not like a pickup line.

Bonnie gave her a tight but still friendly smile. "Not allowed. 'Don't fraternize with the customers.' Thanks for the offer, though. Maybe after I get off some time."

"What time do you usually get off?"

Bonnie shrugged. "About now. Maybe a little later. After it empties out. Usually by four, though."

Laura looked at her watch. "Damn," she said softly. "I have a meeting at four. Maybe we could meet tomorrow. I'll save my coffee break until four and meet you right outside. We could go window shopping at the new Bloomingdale's down the street."

"Can't afford anything there," Bonnie joked. "More like Ross and Target for me."

"No kidding," Laura pressed a little harder. "Me too. We can just look. I can't afford it either. Fun to look, though."

Bonnie tilted her head to one side as if she were considering it. Then she quickly gave in. "Okay. I could use that." She held out her beautiful black hand. "I'm Bonnie."

"I know," Laura laughed softly, pointing to Bonnie's name tag. "I'm Laura. Pleased to meet you, Bonnie."

They arranged to meet the following day, and Laura gulped down half of her coffee and left, too exhilarated and spinning with happy feelings to hang around any longer and be tempted to stare at the darling Bonnie going about her workday chores. She had been so caught up in the thrill of touching Bonnie's hand and making their little date that she completely forgot until she got back upstairs to her office on the thirty-fourth floor that tomorrow she was leaving for Charlotte and would be in the air somewhere over Illinois at the time she and Bonnie had appointed to meet.

Quickly, daring to be late to her four o'clock meeting, she again dashed downstairs to the alley, but the sandwich shop was already closed, darkened, all the chairs stacked upside down on the tables, the coffee urns gleaming, the afternoon shadows deepening along the buildings. She went back to her meeting with the sinking feeling that Bonnie would feel she had been somehow given the brush-off tomorrow, when Laura failed to show up. And yet, they barely knew each other. How could Bonnie feel rejected? I'll just have to patch it up when I get back, Laura thought. She didn't know why it quickly became such a gnawing ache in her, but she did like Bonnie instinctively and looked forward more to a quick window-shopping jaunt with her than any boring business trip to Charlotte.

Bonnie! Oh god! Laura thought. It had now been over two weeks since she had missed her little afternoon 'date' with Bonnie to walk down Market Street to the new Bloomies and stroll through it together, a kind of sweet, friendly intimacy-in-full-view that Laura hoped would lead to something even more intimate, though it was already fairly clear that Bonnie was not inclined that way.

Nevertheless, Laura felt wretched about not having lived up to her end of the deal. As soon as she could break free she dashed down to the sandwich shop in the alley, only to find a new girl working the counter and the register, a neurasthenic looking dishwater blonde with buck teeth and a nasty sneer. To Laura's question about Bonnie she could only say that she knew nothing as it was her first day.

Now Laura's heart sank for sure. God, how will I ever find her again? It was so silly, she realized. They barely knew one another, and here Laura was acting like a devastated lover. She immediately knew the blonde thought of her that way. She slunk away, feeling depressed and ashamed of herself for having delayed so long that Bonnie had slipped away. Without ever knowing the happiness I could bring her, she thought. Without ever feeling my lips against her smooth, dark flesh.

But then Laura realized that she was pretending Bonnie to be the aggrieved one when actually it was her own selfish, stifled lust that was uppermost in her mind. I deserve it, she thought. She did not return to the sandwich shop until the end of the week, and then not to eat but just to take a glimpse, hoping beyond hope that Bonnie would mysteriously reappear.

And even though the blonde was still there, just by chance, before Laura wandered off again, disconsolate and glum, she glimpsed her in the back, behind a swinging door that separated the front of the shop from the rear. Laura wanted to cry out. Bonnie! Oh god, sweet mystery of life I've finally found you! Oh frabjous day! Callooh, callay!

She was wildly, foolishly excited. She tried to get a grip on her feelings. Bonnie seemed more gorgeous to her than usual, though she was, realistically, a fairly ordinary looking girl: attractive but unremarkable. Laura knew she was lathering up this image in her mind of Bonnie as the long-lost girl of her dreams. You foolish thing! she told herself. And you, married to the sweetest woman who ever lived, off there in New York wowing the crowds and totally ignorant of your little sexual adventures! Shame!

But just as she was about to shout, though discreetly, if that were possible, and make a total fool out of herself right there in public, Bonnie saw her too, over the top of the swinging door. Her face lit up with recognition of Laura. Laura waved.

Bonnie came out to her, smiling and friendly. She had, as Laura already knew, a sweet nature and seemed not at all miffed by Laura's missing their 'date.' "Hi," she almost twinkled at Laura, her black eyes shiny and happy. "Long time no see. You been gone somewhere, I can tell."

"I'm so embarrassed. I missed our . . ." Laura had become accustomed to saying 'date' in her mind, but that was so full of innuendo that she dared not say it aloud and didn't know what to substitute in its place.

"Appointment?" Bonnie supplied, without guile or apparent concern. "I just thought you got tied up in something. No big deal."

"It's a big deal to me," Laura confessed. "I feel so bad. I got sent to North Carolina, of all places. I forgot all about telling you until I was actually on the plane."

"You must have a great job," Bonnie beamed. "They just send you off some place like that, without a warning?"

Laura nodded. Since Bonnie seemed impressed—there was no sense in not playing up your assets—she added that the week after that she had flown to New York for a few days. She did not mention Makeeda. Bonnie was relaxed and flexible, but they didn't yet need to get into Laura's private life.

"Well," Bonnie said, after an uncomfortable moment, "I gotta get back to work. No chatting with the customers, remember?"

"I do remember. But I like our chats. Why don't we . . . like . . . have a drink after work. Something like that."

"Don't drink," Bonnie smiled, crinkling her nose. "Only soda."

"They serve soda in bars too," Laura remarked with a wicked smile. "After a day at work, I need something a little stronger."

"I guess I could hang around for a while. I could go up to Bloomingdale's and look around, like we were gonna do."

"Wish I could get away earlier to join you, but I can't. Why don't I meet you there? Around five-thirty."

They agreed to meet at the front entrance, and Laura returned to work, feeling her heart skip and flutter, but knowing there was not a reason in the world to be feeling so exuberant and optimistic. Even though Bonnie was friendly, and very beguiling in her sweet, simple innocence, she still did not register on Laura's sensitivity meter as a likely sexual prospect, a potentially interested party. Oh well. I will still enjoy being in her company for a while, she resigned herself. She is sweet and lovely, and I will restrain myself and simply wish I could fuck her instead of actually doing it.

She met Bonnie at five-thirty and they strolled through Bloomingdale's together, as well as few adjacent stores. "Sure you won't join me for that drink?" Laura prompted. "There's a great bar I know of about two blocks from here."

Bonnie smiled and shook her head. "I should be getting home. I never feel too comfortable in a bar."

"Even with me?"

"I should be getting home."

"Let me give you a ride, at least."

Bonnie consented. She lived in an apartment by Lake Merritt, in Oakland. Laura parked in front, in the white zone, and waited patiently for Bonnie to invite her up, but Bonnie did not. Oh god, I'm losing this little game, Laura thought, almost desperately. When next would she have an opportunity to press things forward? When Bonnie started to get out of the car, Laura risked all.

"Do you suppose I could come in for a second? I have to go to the bathroom."

Bonnie smiled. "Sure. There are a few visitors' parking spaces around to the left. I'll show you."

A few minutes later, when she emerged from the bathroom in Bonnie's small studio apartment (she had run the water and pretended to be going about her business, all the while scheming, her heart fluttering, about how she could now proceed), Bonnie was clattering around in her small kitchen. "Want something to eat? I'm going to cook."

Was this an invitation to dinner? Laura wondered. "I don't want to impose."

"You ain't imposing. I invited you, didn't I?"

I need a drink, Laura thought. The tension is just too great for me. I hate to be the sort who needs a drink, but I might as well be honest. I need one. "I need a drink," she said, almost unconsciously, then instantly grew very ashamed.

Bonnie saw her blushing. "You don't have to blush," she giggled. "Lots of people want a drink at the end of the day." She went to the cupboard. "I have an old bottle of vodka that an old boyfriend left over here. What do you think? Will that do?"

"Only if you'll join me."

Bonnie looked at her as if Laura were, maybe, deaf. "I told you I don't drink."

"I'll feel like the only drunk at a party," Laura complained, now for the first time beginning to relax, to enjoy looking at Bonnie, to see again what she had seen the first time, what had attracted her.

Moving around calmly in her own kitchen, preparing to cook, Bonnie had the sweet, thrilling naturalness of the girl next door Laura had at first seen her to be. She was darkly lovely in her blue golf shirt, her work 'uniform' which she had not changed, her short, shiny black hair curled in scallops around her beautifully-shaped black ears. She had what some people, Laura supposed, would consider big lips, but they were sensual miracles to Laura, who wanted to kiss them forever. And now and then, when Bonnie turned her back, Laura's gaze would drift down speedily to her amazing, swelling bottom, so perfectly encased in her tight blue jeans. But then she would look up quickly again, before Bonnie caught her.

"I don't like the taste," Bonnie said, starting to peel a potato. "You like smothered potatoes? Slum gullion? That's what I call it. Slum gullion. Just potatoes and onions. A little garlic, if you don't mind. Smells, though. Maybe I'll leave it out. And I can chop up some sausage and mix it in. Quick dinner. I do it often."

"I will eat whatever you eat. I consider it a privilege to have been asked."

Bonnie grinned. "You're kidding. It's just onions and potatoes. Okay, I'll have a little drink with you, if you insist. But only a little. And I have to pour it into some Coke because I can't stand the taste."

"Vodka doesn't have much taste."

"It does to me."

In a few more seconds Laura had her vodka over ice and Bonnie an inch or so poured into a tall glass of Coke. They clinked glasses, and Laura actually felt a happy little twinge deep inside her pussy, even though there had been no indication things would ever go further than this. But at least they had got this far.

"To our little stroll through Bloomies," Laura said. "We finally made it."

Bonnie nodded and smiled, making a little face when she sipped her Coke, but only, Laura felt, theatrically, as if she were expected after all she had said not to like it. "Got to tell you, though, I don't know whether I'd buy any of that stuff, even if I could afford it. I just don't go nowhere where you have to dress like that. I'm pretty much a jeans and tee shirt kind of girl, if you know what I mean."

Laura nodded back. "You look great in them."

Suddenly she felt like this was a transparently conniving statement, as if she were flattering Bonnie in order to get to her pussy, which was true, though she didn't want it to seem that way. She was about to blush again until Bonnie abruptly turned away, preoccupied, to the kitchen counter. "I've got to get this stuff going before this vodka you made me drink makes it impossible for me to cook."

"Oh, don't be silly," Laura joked, setting her own drink down. "Let me help you."

She knew that cooking together was another kind of intimacy, one that was even potentially very deep. When you cooked together, it could be a symbolic fucking together, food being as basic as sex. Bonnie looked up at her and smiled in the most thrilling way, a smile Laura could feel down to her toes, though it had not the slightest intimation of sex in it at all.

"You can chop that onion. Don't cut yourself. That knife is sharp. My Daddy taught me how to keep my knives sharp."

Laura took her warning seriously and duly chopped the onion expertly before returning to her drink. "Maybe we both ought to get this done before our little drinkie," she said, feeling suddenly ditzy and foolish for talking in near-babytalk, as if she were so giddy and flirtatious here in Bonnie's tiny kitchen that she could not control herself. And she hadn't even had more than a sip of her vodka yet.

Bonnie said nothing but continued peeling and chopping potatoes, then frying up the lot of it in a huge skillet. "Hope you getting hungry," she said.

"The smell of it alone is enough to make me ravenous," Laura acknowledged.

Bonnie turned the heat way down and covered the skillet with a large lid. Then she picked up her tall, vodka-laced Coke. Laura was startled to notice, as if for the first time, that one thing that made Bonnie's face so enchanting was her high cheekbones. Because her face was not gaunt or especially long, you did not notice it at first, but the more you scrutinized it, the more you realized that she had prominent high cheekbones that somehow made her face very striking.

"God, I never noticed until now your beautiful high cheekbones," she said as they moved from the tiny kitchen into Bonnie's tiny living room/bedroom combination.

"One of my great grandmothers was a full-blooded Choctaw Indian," Bonnie said. "Guess that's where I get it. Hair, too." She fluffed her short, jet black hair with her fingers. "This dense, clumpy mix of Indian and black hair."

"I think your hair is beautiful," Laura said, sounding almost prim to herself. Tea party conversation. "It frames those cheekbones. Makes you exotic."

Bonnie giggled softly. "You think I'm exotic?"

Laura looked deep into her eyes. "I don't know. I barely know you."

"You better be careful, Laura," Bonnie laughed softly. "I got girlfriends who would think you're a lesbian when you talk like that."

Laura didn't say anything. She didn't know whether to simply admit it right now and get it over with, or to continue to skirt around her increasingly strong desires. It was hard to sit here with the enchanting Bonnie and keep denying her growing desire to touch her. To touch her everywhere. She wondered if it showed in her face. After all, Bonnie could be making this casual joke about Laura being a lesbian without even realizing that she was speaking the truth of some deeper-seated understanding. She could be picking up from Laura the deeper vibrations of Laura's physical desire.

They were sitting at opposite ends of a large navy blue sofa, which Laura figured must double as Bonnie's bed a night. There was no other bed in sight, and no other room for one to be concealed in. Why don't we just roll this baby out and lie down together on it? she wanted to say to the delicious girl.

"But I guess you couldn't be one with that ring you got," Bonnie went on, pointing to the gold band on Laura's finger.

Laura held up her hand and twisted it in the light. Both of them looked at the gold ring. "What if I were married . . . to someone else?" Laura said boldly. "You know . . . not a man."

"You mean, married to a woman?" Bonnie laughed. "Like those people on the news?"

Laura nodded and smiled.

Bonnie looked away but didn't flinch. "I got a girlfriend who's a lesbian," she said, in a soft, barely audible voice. "I mean, we're not girlfriends in that way," she looked directly into Laura's eyes as she said this, "but she is one. All of us just sort of accept it. Her friends. She doesn't try to do any of us. At least I don't think so. She never did try to do me, anyway."

Bonnie, Laura realized, was nervous. That was why she was rattling on this way.

"Maybe you're not her type," Laura said, also softly, not taking her eyes from Bonnie's. You're my type, though, she let her eyes say, made them even pulse this message. You are really my type. You are my type to the nth degree. I want you so much.

"Anyway," Bonnie continued nervously, "even if you were . . . like, married to a girl, you'd be cheating on her if you . . . you know, made a pass at me."

"Am I making a pass at you?"

Bonnie squirmed and looked away. "I . . . don't think so."

Laura smiled. "I think your lesbian girlfriend has very poor taste if she hasn't come on to you," she said evenly, without inflection.

Bonnie giggled nervously. "Why do you think that?"

"Those high cheekbones would get me in a minute," Laura continued smiling.

Now there was a painful silence. Things had in only seconds become abundantly clear, and Bonnie appeared to be digesting their implications. Then she hopped off the sofa. "Oh shit, I forgot the potatoes!"

Laura was right behind her as she dashed to the little kitchen. Fortunately, the slum gullion was not ruined, only on the verge of being ruined. "Sorry I distracted you," Laura apologized as Bonnie scooped it from the skillet into a serving dish. "I can . . . leave, if you like."

Bonnie looked miffed. "I invited you, didn't I?" she said again. "Sit down."

They ate in silence. The food was very good. "You are a very good cook, Bonnie. How did you do this with only potatoes and onions?"

Bonnie shrugged. "My Mama taught me. Glad you like it."

Laura tried hard not to flirt any more. It was pretty clear that flirting would not get her what she wanted, and it only made things more painful to them both. She finished her plate and her vodka, then folded her napkin. "Well, guess I'd better be going. Don't want to interfere with your evening."

Bonnie, across the table, looked almost forlorn, as if she didn't want Laura to leave and also did want her to go at the same time. It was as if nothing was settled between them, which was actually a good sign to Laura. Maybe she'll start thinking about her girlfriend the lesbian, and me the lesbian, and how she's sitting home alone here while she could be with either of us. Especially me. Maybe I should leave her my phone number.

"You have far to go?" Bonnie asked.

Laura shook her head. "I live in Berkeley. Just about five minutes from here."

"With your . . . wife? Is that what you call her?" Bonnie asked diffidently.

Laura smiled, now very relaxed since the pressure was off. They weren't going to fuck, probably ever, so at least she could be calm and friendly. "Actually, I do call her that, in my mind."

"Maybe she'll be disappointed that you had dinner here."

"She's in New York. She's . . . working there. She's a singer. Jazz. Cabaret. She won't be home for a few more days."

They talked in the same desultory fashion for another twenty minutes or so. Then Laura stood up to leave. "You know," she said at the door, "if I promise not to make a pass at you, could you give me your phone number? We don't really have any way to reach one another unless I come down to your shop."

Bonnie agreed and they exchanged numbers. She looked wistfully at Laura. "I like you, Laura. I kind of even wish I was that way . . . so we could spend a little more time together."

Laura leaned forward and kissed her smooth black forehead. She then tenderly caressed one enchanting high cheekbone with her fingertip. "You just keep thinking that way and call me now and then," she murmured.

She awoke in the middle of the night. Monk and Mingus, the two cats, were sleeping on the bed with her, and they briefly, drowsily, awakened too, offering their quiet reassurances. Makeeda was in Japan again, having flown there only weeks after her New York engagement, appearing at a regional jazz festival followed by two weeks appearing at a Tokyo club. The Japanese had an insatiable appetite for jazz, and Makeeda was better known and more popular there than at home.

Laura had awakened in the dark because in her dreams she suddenly became certain that she did not know Bonnie's last name. After all this flirtation, and even their disappointing little dinner in Bonnie's apartment, even the exchange of phone numbers, they had not told each other their last names. Laura was sure of it.

Not that it mattered. Even the dream she had had was not a sexual dream, for some reason. Bonnie was in it, but only as a member of a crowd, an anonymous crowd, and Laura could not remember what she, Bonnie, had been doing, if anything. Still, it troubled her very much not to know Bonnie's last name, and she made it a point on the next day to go to the sandwich shop in the alley for lunch.

"I realized I don't know your last name," she said to Bonnie as she was paying for her sandwich.

Bonnie gave her a smile, unexpectedly, that warmed Laura's heart and streamed from there directly down to the deep place in her pussy where she harbored her secret sexual longings. And yet, she reminded herself, it was the smile Bonnie gave everyone, as she deposited the change in their palms, letting her fingertips linger there momentarily in that sweet, intimate gesture that Laura had initially thought was just for her until she saw Bonnie doing it with everybody in line.

"Holland," Bonnie said, still smiling. "You know, like the country. Yours is . . . Roberts?"

"Robbins. Did I tell you?"

Bonnie nodded. She leaned close. "Better move on. I gotta get to these folks." With her head she indicated the people behind Laura in the line.

"Of course. Sorry."

Again, there was no time or opportunity to go any further. Laura was glum but resigned. It had been two weeks since she had given Bonnie her phone number, her work number of course, and yet Bonnie had not called. Somebody else, some man, alas, was going to get his hands on that sweet girl's sweet body before Laura ever would.

And Laura stewed and simmered. For days. Bonnie never called her. After all, I've given her every chance, Laura thought. I didn't even push it. That time when I went down there to the alley to find out her last name, I didn't even push it. I didn't even suggest we get together. Nothing. You'd think if she had a little interest, even a little, that she would phone. Just for a coffee date or something.

But she also realized that Bonnie was shy. She was not like LaVonda: feverishly curious and eager. Instead, the knowledge that Laura might desire her sexually had made Bonnie nervous and withdrawn. A part of her nature might want it to go on, might want Laura to make further advances, but her general wariness would not allow it.

That's it, I'm just going to have to draw her out, Laura thought. It's up to me. If I wait, she'll never call. I'm going to have to risk the whole thing, just to get her attention.

Just when she became resolutely determined to march down to the alley sandwich shop that very afternoon and boldly ask Bonnie to dinner, or to a movie, or to go for a nice evening stroll around Lake Merritt, she got a call from her on her cell phone. "Bonnie? Oh god, you called!" Laura let this slip out before she realized that it wasn't exactly wise since her exclamation made it seem like she was sitting on the edge of her chair waiting for Bonnie to call.

Bonnie was shy, fulfilling Laura's prophecies. Her voice was barely audible. She wasn't shy when she was doing her job, nor had she been when Laura had eaten dinner with her in her apartment. But now that the terms of their relationship had altered, now that she knew why Laura was attracted to her, that it was physical as well as friendly, she was shy. "Cooking tonight. More slum gullion. Thought you might want to have dinner."

If someone offered me a million bucks, I wouldn't want it more, Laura's inner voice was crowing happily. But she restrained her delivery. "Why . . . I think that would be wonderful. If you can hang around until about five-thirty I could give you a ride."

Bonnie snorted and snuffled nervously. "I don't think so. That's an hour and a half. I could be home by then on the bus. I could already be cooking. Why don't you just come by when you get off."

Laura smiled. I can't wait, my darling. "I'll be there with bells on," she said brightly. She didn't know exactly what that meant, but her mother always said it.

And somehow this brightened Bonnie's mood; maybe her mother always said it too; or maybe it was simply that Laura had accepted her invitation. She was upbeat. "Good. I'll get down that bottle of vodka and have it ready for you."

Laura clucked into the phone. "Bonnie! You act like I'm a closet tippler or something."

"Only kidding." This easy badinage was thrilling to Laura, and she guessed it might be to Bonnie too. "See you then."

She stopped on her way to the parking garage to her car and bought half a dozen yellow roses. She did not buy red since that might seem inappropriately romantic somehow, but yellow seemed okay. And yet, when she got there she left them in the car. Bonnie was too sweet and unpretentious, and also clearly a little nervous about this invitation, and Laura figured that underlining it with a gift of flowers would be too brazen, as if she were saying "Okay, girl, let's get on with it. You know what I want."

That was too crude and too rude. This, on her way up the elevator, made her grin as it reminded her of the old limerick about a guy named McGruder who liked his girl nude when he screwed her. She giggled softly to herself and carefully composed her face into a mask of pleasant friendliness, banishing such crass rhymes completely from her mind before knocking on Bonnie's door.

Bonnie greeted her wearing an apron that said: Even Cowgirls Get the Blues. Laura could not suppress a grin. This was a side of Bonnie, evidently, that she had not seen.

"Love your apron."

Bonnie squinted bashfully. "My sister gave it to me. She got it at a yard sale and decided it really fit me. I don't even know what a cowgirl is."

Mmmmm, Laura thought, maybe we can remedy that, darling. She thought quickly of Allisha, who especially among all Laura's lovers liked getting 'cowgirl rammed,' as she called it. But she quickly banished such thoughts. Bonnie was more fetching than ever in her cute apron. She still wore her blue polo shirt, her work 'uniform,' under it.

"Mmmmm, that smell is delicious," Laura smiled. "I see you've been busy while I've been stuck in traffic."

"It's all ready. I'm just keeping it warm."

Now there was a moment of discomfort for them both. They looked at each other and didn't know what to do next. The uncomfortable pause was fraught with the knowledge of what had passed between them here before, and what this reunion must mean. We're going to do it, Laura realized. Otherwise she never would have invited me here. The problem is, how do we get there. She is willing to do it but is leaving the rest up to me.

"I guess maybe I'll take that drink, if you're still offering it," Laura smiled gently.

"Oh. Right. I forgot." Bonnie turned to her small kitchen. "Vodka and ice? I got some Sprite."

"Just a little splash of Sprite will be okay. You're joining me, aren't you? Remember . . . I don't want to be the only drunk at the party."

Bonnie poured the drinks very methodically, giving herself a tall glass of Coke with a little vodka in it. "Can't stand the taste," she reminded Laura.

Laura came up behind her, before Bonnie could reach for the full glasses and hand her one. She put one hand on Bonnie's shoulder. "Here," she murmured softly, "let me help you off with the apron."

Bonnie turned to look back at Laura over her shoulder. Her dark eyes were shiny with expectation, and their eyes locked together as Laura loosened the knot holding the apron on, then undid it completely. "Thank you," she said, her voice barely audible.

She pulled the neck string over her head and tossed the apron into a kitchen chair, a kind of symbolic disrobing. Again Laura touched her arm before she could return to the drinks on the tile sink board. She raised her fingertips to Bonnie's lovely face and brushed her cheek with them. "Thank you for inviting me," she whispered.

Bonnie smiled. "I guess you better kiss me if you're going to do it," she said. "I'm getting real nervous waiting."

Laura smiled. "That makes two of us." She dropped her fingertips to Bonnie's full lips, thick and pillowy and inviting, umber-colored with no lipstick. "Guess I will . . . and put an end to the suspense."

She slid her fingers to the side, caressing Bonnie's smooth black cheek again, and moved her face closer, brushing Bonnie's lips with her own. Laura knew from experience how to make it a very slow and romantic first kiss, and Bonnie helped by tilting her head a little to the side so that their mouths melted more easily together. Neither opened her mouth at first, being content to press her lips to the other's mouth lightly but expressively. Then Laura slowly but surely began to insinuate the tip of her tongue between Bonnie's lips, and Bonnie obligingly parted them to let it in.

Up to this point only their lips touched, and now their tongues, as well as Laura's fingertips still caressing Bonnie's cheek. But slowly, as the lengthy kiss wore on, they began to press the rest of their bodies together, and Laura's arms slowly encircled Bonnie, until she was holding her close and kissing her more hungrily. And wonder of wonders, Bonnie was kissing back.

She began to kiss Laura back heatedly. This poor darling girl is hungry for love, Laura thought, ratcheting up the heat a little more herself. Shoot, I just should have pressed it the first time. She probably would've given in. She wants to be kissed like this.

When they stopped for a moment, Laura kept kissing her face. "Your skin is so smooth . . . and beautiful," she panted softly, kissing Bonnie's high cheek bones. "I love your Choctaw Indian cheek bones."

Bonnie giggled softly, demurely. "You crazy, Laura."

Laura stopped her bashful giggling with another passionate kiss. Again Bonnie kissed back hungrily. Laura's fingers bit into the resilient flesh of Bonnie's back through her shirt. She slithered her tongue deep into Bonnie's mouth. Bonnie responded by drilling hers deep into Laura's. They were both panting when they broke off the kiss.

"I think we should . . . sit down on the sofa," Laura panted.

Bonnie winked and crooked her finger. She took Laura's hand and drew her over to the wall furthest from the kitchen, swiveling the panel to expose the large Murphy bed behind it. She caught Laura's glance with a significant flash of her dark eyes. Then she carefully lowered the bed and pulled down the blanket.

Laura was so thrilled by this gesture that she could barely speak. This girl means to pull me down on this bed and fuck me, she thought playfully, feeling her heart race and her blood surge. She took Bonnie's hand and raised it to her lips, this hand that had lingered so often in hers when giving her change for a sandwich, the slim, tapered black fingers that had made her heart leap and her pussy throb.

"Kiss me again," she murmured, not knowing what else to say at this moment, this very significant moment. Bringing the bed out could have only one meaning, and she was electrified at Bonnie's boldness.

She kissed her mouth and her smooth black neck and her shiny black ear, nuzzling her hair, digging her fingers into the hard round resilience of Bonnie's ass—that spectacular ass!— through her jeans for the very first time. Though not as obsidian-dark as Dee Dee or Dawn, for example, Bonnie was darker than LaVonda, whom Laura had most recently been nuzzling, and as usual Laura found her delicious black skin a huge erotic turn-on. Bonnie passively accepted Laura's acute physical hunger, letting herself be kissed and caressed, but finally pulling back to pose a sensible question.

"You want to do this first or eat first? If we're not going to eat, I've got to turn off the fire under the slum gullion."

Laura leaned forward and kissed her forehead. "I want you more than I want food. I want to eat you alive."

Bonnie broke into an embarrassed grin, as if she were ashamed to admit that she wanted the same thing. "I'll be right back. Don't move."

"I won't."

Bonnie turned off the fire on the stove and returned quickly to Laura to turn up the fire there. "What do we do now, get undressed?"

"Well . . ." Laura pretended to think it over. "It's usually easier when you're undressed. Not always, but usually. I think . . . we should help each other undress. Me first. I'll help you out of these jeans."

She slowly ran down the zipper of Bonnie's tight blue jeans, then eased them over her hips and down her sleek black thighs. She knelt while doing this and could not resist pressing her lips to the hard sleek flesh. True to her word, Bonnie was a simple girl and wore simple white cotton underpants, which Laura, after getting the girl's ankles free of her blue jeans, quickly got her hands under. She could not wait to fill her hands with Bonnie's round, firm buns, which she had been lusting after for months, it seemed.

"You know, you have a beautiful ass," she murmured, standing again to face Bonnie, but keeping her hands under Bonnie's panties, happily clutching the hard round moons.

Bonnie grinned and nodded. "People look at it a lot."

"People want to do this," Laura whispered, squeezing them. "If they're like me they want to kiss it all over."

"You want to do that?"

"Oh yes. God, yes."

"Guys want to stick their dicks in it."

Laura kissed her neck, unbuttoning the top button of Bonnie's golf shirt. "You let them?"

Bonnie shook her head. "Too big."

"Mmmmm, maybe a finger would feel better."

Bonnie frowned, but not with hostility. "I don't know about that."

"Can we take this off too?" Laura suggested, plucking at the bottom of the blue shirt.

Bonnie shook her head playfully, grinning like a school girl. "I ain't going to be the only one naked here, any more than you're going to be the only drunk at the party."

"You're right," Laura smiled back, quickly removing her blouse, and unfastening her skirt, letting it fall around her feet. She was so eager to be naked with Bonnie, after all this time waiting for it, that she didn't even bother to carefully fold up her clothes. "Now you."

Now Bonnie flirted. Even though she was genuinely a shy, natural, girl-next-door type who seemed usually oblivious to her very real charms, she also had a streak of coquetry that was irresistible. She removed the blue polo shirt as if she had practiced every move, from the tantalizing lift of the bottom of it to slowly reveal the delicious black skin of her taut midriff, to the slow pulling of the collar over her short black hair. She wore a simple white bra underneath it, matching her simple cotton underpants.

She was a vision. Alluring, lacy underwear like Laura's could hardly have made her sexier. Now they were both down to bra and panties. Bonnie, Laura was delighted to see, could not keep her eyes off Laura's near-naked body any more than Laura could keep her eyes from devouring Bonnie's. Bonnie touched Laura's lacy champagne-colored bra with one finger.

"This is the kind of bra they had at Bloomies when we went there," she said, her eyes wide, admiring it. "I never had one like it."

Laura kissed her gleaming black shoulder, running her lips along it up Bonnie's neck. "You don't need one like this. With the body you've got, a bra is just an irrelevance."

Bonnie grinned, delighted to be so praised. "You think so?"

Laura nodded. "I think so. The first time I saw you, I said to myself 'I've got to have that girl. God, she's lovely. She may not sleep with girls, but I'm sure going to try.'"

"See? You were right to keep trying."

Now Laura embraced her again and kissed her while unfastening her bra behind her back with the fingers of both hands as they kissed. "I guess I was. I didn't know whether you'd ever give in, though."

She skimmed the loose straps down Bonnie's long arms, and Bonnie flung the bra across the room into a chair, her firm naked breasts jiggling only slightly. She looked down at Laura's pale hands that quickly scooped them up. They were perfectly shaped and round and high upswept balls, with medium sized black nipples that were swollen and a little shiny.

"Look at our skins together," Bonnie said softly, in wonderment. "Here . . . take yours off too."

She helped Laura off with her bra, as Laura had done for her. Now she put her slim dark hands on Laura's small naked breasts. They kissed, holding each other's breasts, squeezing, kneading.

"Wow," Bonnie gasped against Laura's cheek, "this is a lot different than making it with a guy."

Laura smiled, kissing her again, unable to get enough. "How do you think?"

"I don't know. Slow. Gentle. Real exciting. I like watching our skins together. I like kissing you . . . and feeling you. Your body . . . against mine like this."

"Shall we lie down on the bed?"

"I guess we better if we're going to go on with this," Bonnie grinned.

"I love your boobs . . . they're so beautiful," Laura murmured as she and Bonnie lay down face to face on the bed. Laura held the lovely round globes in her hands. "They're high . . . like your cheek bones."

"Guess I'm just high all over," Bonnie giggled softly. "Except in the head. I didn't even have a sip of that drink. We just got to . . . doing this . . . so fast."

Laura kissed her neck and shoulders, dropping her mouth now to Bonnie's firm little breasts, tonguing and sucking one beautiful nipple. "I'm drunk on you, I don't need anything else," she murmured.

"Ohhhhh. Mmmmm, that feels good," Bonnie panted softly.

Laura did not reply but began a full-scale love assault on Bonnie's delectable breasts. She held them both in her hands, reluctant to spend attention on one at the expense of the other, and so squeezing them both and moving her hungry mouth from one shiny, saliva-wet black nipple to the other one, sucking them, lip-biting them, stabbing them with her tongue, then sucking them harder, so hard in fact that Bonnie shuddered and rose up off the mattress, keening deep in her throat.

"Unnggeeeee! Ohmmm! Unggeee! Oh shit . . . that's hard!"

"Oh, I'm sorry, honey, is that too hard?" Laura asked, sliding up and kissing her face, very concerned.

Bonnie's face modulated from a sharp grimace into a smile. "Oh no. It kinda felt good. I just wasn't expecting it. Nobody ever did that to me before."

"Sucked you?"

"Just that hard."

Laura gave her a contrite smile. "I get a little carried away."

Bonnie tittered softly. "You should feel how wet it made me. You did that and I started to gushing."

"Mmmm," Laura grinned, "guess I better find out." She trailed one hand down Bonnie's silky black body toward her crotch, but Bonnie grabbed it before it could reach its destination.

"Not yet," she said, charmingly pliant and warm and affectionate. "Let's kiss again a little. And push together, like this. I like to feel your body against me like this. And my titties are all wet now. They'll stick to yours."

"I hope they do," Laura said, embracing her and mashing their naked breasts together, kissing her again passionately.

"What do you call this?" Bonnie said quietly after a while, after more kissing and rubbing. "You call it fucking? I mean what we're doing. What we're going to do. It really ain't fucking, is it? Like, I think of fucking as . . . well, you have to have a stiff dick going in and out of you. Right?"

"Mmmmm, who cares what you call it when it feels so good," Laura murmured, burying her face in Bonnie's sweet black neck and running her hands up to her high, firm breasts. "I want to suck your nipples again and make you pant."

"You're already doing that," Bonnie smiled. "The panting part. This feels so great. Can I suck yours a little?"

"God, you can do anything you want to me, honey."

Bonnie kissed her way down Laura's bare shoulder and upper chest to her small, perfect breasts, holding them in her slim dark hands and examining them closely. "Yours are so . . . beautiful."

She paused before saying it, as if finding the right word were difficult. But then she began kissing and sucking one as if she had done it all her life. Laura relaxed and let the warm, sensual feelings flow through her body. "You're good at this," she whispered, caressing Bonnie's forehead.

Bonnie grinned up at her. "Beginner's luck. You like it?"

"I love it. Do it harder."

"You like it that way too?" Bonnie began to suck Laura's nipples aggressively, as Laura had sucked hers, going back and forth between them, and squeezing Laura's breasts passionately.

In only a few moments Laura was writhing and mewling. "Oh Jesus . . . that feels so good!" she panted to Bonnie.

Her hands flittered over every part of Bonnie's smooth, naked body that they could reach, then pulled her up so she could kiss her mouth again. There was no substitute for a deep, searing soul kiss.

"Whatever you call it, I want to do it!" she panted to Bonnie. "I want your beautiful pussy."

Bonnie snickered. "You all wet and hot too, like me," she smiled.

"Yes."

"I guess you'll have to show me what comes next. I've never done this."

Laura kissed her nose. "I think you may have done it in another life. You're very good at it."

"You're going to make me blush."

Laura was already devouring her. Bonnie did not have a body like LaVonda's or Makeeda's, statuesque, voluptuous—few women did; God knows I don't, Laura thought—but it was nevertheless quite beautiful in its own way, very well-proportioned and sleek and dark and curvaceous, and Laura could not keep her hands or mouth off any of it. Especially that miracle ass. Give me that beautiful ass, darling.

She maneuvered Bonnie onto her stomach and began the supremely enjoyable task of making love to this hall of fame bottom. She knew this was their first time, and Bonnie was proud of her ass but not yet into anal sex, and so her attentions had to be limited to kneading, kissing, gently biting, and other non-invasive caresses, but that was certainly enough for the present, and she spent a good five minutes lavishing an extraordinary amount of skilled lechery on these marvelous twin black moons.

For her part, Bonnie enjoyed every second. She squirmed and clenched her firm round buns, and panted and giggled and squirmed some more, tensing up only briefly when Laura's tongue snaked in between the hard bubbles, into the dark secret crease between them, which was extra deep because of the firm swelling mounds.

"Ooohhhh! Ooohhhh shit . . . that feels . . . that tickles! Ummnnggghhh! Oh shit, it feels good too!"

"You like that? You want me to stop?"

"Don't stop! Unhhhhh! Oh shit, that feels good."

"Oh Bonnie, you are so lovely. I dreamed of this. I looked at you in the sandwich shop and dreamed of kissing your wonderful ass all over like this."

"You did?" Bonnie lifted her cheek off the mattress and looked back over her shoulder at Laura, in disbelief. "You really did?"

"God, yes. I wanted to touch you. I quivered inside with the need to touch you. I wanted to kiss you all over your body, and especially your beautiful ass. Like this."

Bonnie grinned. She plopped her face down on the sheet again and gyrated her pretty ass suggestively up and back into Laura's face. "I never knew," she said happily. "I never knew you wanted to do that."

Laura went on kissing it, but it became harder and harder for her to ignore the sweet, puckered, festering wet pussy just below Bonnie's curvy black moons. The wonderful pungent odor alone, the odor of female in heat, was enough to curl her toes and fill her body with sharp lust. She rolled Bonnie over gently and began to lick it.

"Unh! Unh!" Bonnie gasped immediately, very aroused by Laura's passionate attack. "Oh! Oh shit!"

It was a beautiful small tight pussy, not at all like LaVonda's almost extravagantly opulent, floppy-lipped black orchid of a pussy that Laura had lately been hungrily slurping but instead a neat little slot of tight black cunt lips enclosing a fragrant pink trench of glistening wet cunt meat. Even though it was already puckering, Laura pulled it fully open gently with her thumbs and began tonguing and sucking it with concentrated skill, searching out Bonnie's little clit under its hood at the top and stabbing it repeatedly with the tip of her tongue. Bonnie shuddered and moaned.

"Ohhh! Ohnnnnnnn!"

Laura tongued and sucked her more passionately, now introducing two fingers into the soupy furrow of her pussy, fucking her gently and rhythmically with them, bringing her slowly up to the bursting point. Bonnie's sleek, undulating black body was enchanting to her, and when she began to clutch at her own breasts, pulling and squeezing them, Laura knew she was getting closer. Surprisingly, she noticed that she now had three fingers in Bonnie's tight little pussy, and they were sliding in and out with ease.

Bonnie had a snug but very wet and slippery pussy, and she seemed to be responding so excitedly to Laura's probing that Laura was inclined to be even more aggressive. In seconds she had four fingers, then a wedge of five, in Bonnie's yielding slit, pushing, rotating, probing, funneling in. In the beginning she had had not the slightest intention of doing this, but before either of them knew it Laura's hand was completely inside Bonnie's tight pussy, and Bonnie was grimacing and wincing and moaning in intense pleasure, as well as disbelief.

"Ahhhnnnnnnn! Oh! Unngghhh! Ahhnnnnn! Oh . . . shit!"

She looked down, her face contorted in awe and shocking sexual pleasure as she saw Laura's arm from the wrist up protruding from her distended pussy. But the sensations were clearly almost too intense to bear.

"Unnnngghhhhh!" Her hands rose up over her head to clutch the pillow behind her, and her eyes rolled up. Her back arched and her lovely breasts swirled. Her crooked elbows danced in the air above her forehead as she clawed the pillow. "Unnggghhhh! Oh!"

Part of Laura wondered if this was going too far. Fist-fucking a girl, a sweet, natural girl like Bonnie, during their very first moments together in bed, even if they had not planned it, seemed like pushing the envelope. I shouldn't be doing this. I should take my hand out and just suck her and make her come quickly. Then apologize.

But when she looked into Bonnie's blazing, beseeching dark eyes, she knew Bonnie did not want her to stop. Bonnie was becoming more desperate and delirious with need by the second, now slowly gyrating her hips, as if to coax Laura into fist-fucking her more rapidly, more vigorously, instead of just pausing indecisively like this.

She wants me to go on, Laura realized. She's going to come. She'll hate me if I stop now. Oh honey! I want you to come. I want you to come so hard! Your first time with me. Come hard, okay? You can come really hard this way.

She kept up a steady, relentless, slow sliding with her hand, sliding it in and out of the tight, slippery crevice, and Bonnie accordingly fell into the slow, demonic, rhythmical gyration of it, now moaning almost constantly, her eyes locked with Laura's. Both of them, Laura knew, were beginning to fall into that deep, intimate shared trance that mysteriously often accompanied fist-fucking, as if no more stirring connection were possible between two women, and a life-altering orgasm was about to occur.

And Laura realized that it might. At first Bonnie settled into the slow rhythm set by Laura's deliberate thrusting, but before thirty seconds or so she was churning and flexing more urgently, grimacing with need, her moans descending into low, guttural grunts and growls, punctuated by high-pitched whimpering. It was all so desperately erotic that Laura too found herself yearning and pulsing with the need to come, to finish it, to explode, to merge with Bonnie in a conflagration of shrieking orgasms.

"Unnmmgghhh! Mmmmnnuuungggg! Oh! Auummnnggghh!" Bonnie moaned, her lovely black body now glistening with a thin film of sweat as she and Laura both labored toward her fierce final moment.

At one point she reached up frantically with one hand and gripped Laura behind the neck, pulling Laura's head down and craning up at the same time to kiss her. Their mouths met and clashed in heated, clumsy passion, their tongues snaking out, and their breath harsh and rapid. Bonnie gyrated her hips and drove her pussy down on Laura's hand and wrist, pumping hard, so hard that they could not keep kissing.

Her hand dropped from behind Laura's neck to Laura's forearm, just above where her wrist protruded from Bonnie's impaled pussy. With a maniacal, desperate look streaking her dark eyes, she grabbed Laura's arm hard and bore down with her pubic bone, now not so much pumping but furiously jamming her cunt into Laura's hand, rocking, surging, gurgling and gasping crazily. Then, to Laura's shocked amazement, her fingers dug into the flesh of Laura's arm and she began pulling Laura's hand in and out of her pussy almost violently, fucking herself with it almost as if Laura were not attached.

"Nnnngggggg! Ohhhmmnnggg! Nuunngggg!"

From here, of course, the end was not far off. Bonnie groaned, grabbed one delectable swirling breast with her free hand, arched her back, and came in a delirious frenzy.

"AUUNNMMMGGGNNHIIIEEEEEE! UMMNNGGG! ANNGGHHH!"

Laura ran her own free hand up to Bonnie's other breast, cupping and squeezing it while Bonnie's shuddering body went into sharp convulsions of killing pleasure. She had known the girl would come hard, indeed had hoped Bonnie would come very hard, and yet the full force of this shocking orgasm overwhelmed her. And that could not even describe the effect it had on Bonnie, who seemed briefly destroyed by the whole thing, crushed, before stretching and flexing and rolling half onto her side, her arm over her face, which was obscured from Laura's view, her body still undulating and twitching helplessly through the last devastating spasms of a horrific climax.

Laura's hand was still inside of Bonnie's squeezing pussy. She could still feel the contractions of Bonnie's waning orgasm. Bonnie was silently swooning, and Laura did not want to disturb her pleasure, her bliss, which was she reasoned still pretty intense. But after a few moments she did slowly slide her hand out. Bonnie was still very well lubricated, and it slid out easily. Laura wiped it on the edge of the sheet and scooted up to embrace her.

She realized that this was a more shocking initiation into the pleasures of lesbian sex than either had counted on for Bonnie. She barely responded to Laura's kisses, but a smile of excruciating, even excoriating pleasure remained locked on her face. Laura pushed closer, wildly horny herself, she realized, in great need of a release, and thrilled all over by the feel of Bonnie's sleek, naked flesh pressing against her own.

"Ohhhhnnnnn!" Bonnie finally emitted another moan, the first sound she had made in minutes, shifting slightly as she felt Laura's body pressing against her, moving to make it easier, to accept Laura's pushing. Her eyelids fluttered open. "Oh Laura."

By this time Laura had locked her own thighs almost instinctively around one of Bonnie's and was slowly but quite desperately rubbing her pussy up and down on the hard muscle.

"Oh Laura," Bonnie repeated, her eyes questioning, then falling down to Laura's crotch rubbing heatedly against her thigh muscle.

"Just . . . hold on . . . for . . . a . . . second . . ." Laura panted to her, biting her lower lip, grimacing, pumping, already feeling the spark ignite, feeling the hot certain explosion hurtling toward its culmination deep inside her body. "Oh yes! Oh Bonnie . . ."

"Oh Laura." Bonnie's arms encircled her, pulling her even closer, Bonnie's fingers biting into her flesh. "Oh Laura . . . yes!"

"Auunngghhmmmnniieee!" Laura squealed into her neck, coming quickly and sharply, feeling the honeyfire boil up inside her belly and force her body to clench and judder.

"Oh yes . . . oh yes!" Bonnie panted in sympathy with Laura's orgasm, clutching her, holding her, until Laura's sharp quivering began to die away.

The release made Laura giddy. And wildly happy. She could not suppress her laughter. "Well . . . I guess that took care of my problem."

Bonnie joined in the soft laughter. "Took care of mine, too. Shit, I never knew it was even possible to come like that."

"Oh, you like that, do you?" Laura teased her, now regaining enough of her senses to kiss her again. "You little pervert." She tickled Bonnie's ribs. "I usually make my girlfriends wait at least until the second time to get the fist."

"Then I'm lucky, I guess," Bonnie said, solemnly.

"I'm kidding!" Laura tickled her again. "That happened completely by accident. I didn't plan it. It just sort of . . . happened."

"Then I'm glad it did," Bonnie beamed. "I thought I was gonna cum forever."

Laura hugged her tightly, luxuriating in the feel of their naked breasts squishing together. "I thought you were too. I was afraid to move."

They indulged themselves in a long, leisurely, sensual kiss. Laura's fingers again could not stay away from Bonnie's delectable round ass, and she stroked it lovingly but not in any sexually aggressive way, realizing that there would be plenty of time for that.

"I don't know about you, but fucking makes me hella hungry," Bonnie finally whispered against her cheek.

Oh god. Laura's eyes rolled up playfully. Another Dawn. Fuck like a bunny. Then eat like a goat. "It makes me hungry for more of your beautiful pussy," she said, kissing Bonnie's nose. "But I guess I'll have to wait. I somehow have the feeling you mean that delicious-smelling slum gullion over there on the stove."

Bonnie nodded, smiling. "We gotta feed these bodies so they'll be up to what we put them through afterward."

"Oooohhhhhh!" Laura giggled, rolling off the bed after Bonnie. "That sounds like a promise."

Bonnie flung her a thin little nightshirt from the closet behind the Murphy bed, slipping into a similar one herself. She actually flirted with Laura as Laura slipped into hers. "I actually think I could do that again," she said, shyly. "You think I'm a sex maniac?"

Laura grabbed her and kissed her again before she could escape to the small kitchen. "If you are, then I know just the cure."

Bonnie grew kittenish in her arms, still shy and flirtatious. "You gonna fist-fuck me again?"

"Only if you want."

Without answering, Bonnie smiled in a deep, mysterious, and ultimately devastating way. "Let's eat."

To be continued...

Miranda Mars

Little Sex Bunny

Bonnie Chronicles 2

Erotic Lesbian Romance

Bonnie lay face down, dozing, on the Murphy bed, with Laura stretched out beside her, lazily caressing—and now and then leaning over to kiss—her long smooth dark back, and the incredible high sculptured black moons of her lovely bottom. She smiled, feeling Laura's fingertips, occasionally Laura's lips, on her flesh.

"You, my darling," Laura purred, "have the most beautiful back and bottom in creation."

Bonnie smiled and opened her eyes but did not move her head off the sheet. "You think every part of me is beautiful," she said, drowsily. "How can I believe you? I'm just a poor little pickaninny who works in a sandwich shop. How can I be beautiful? How come I ain't in the movies if I'm so beautiful?"

There wasn't much time to reflect at this moment, since Laura did feel an urgent need to quickly plug this hole in Bonnie's self-esteem. But she did have a flash of realization that she had gone from the bed of a jet-set wonder, who had everything, Amber Grant, to the Murphy bed of a sweet and simple girl who probably earned only a smidgen of what she, Laura, even earned in a year. And the basic truth was that you would never hear Amber Grant refer to herself as a 'pickaninny,' that was for sure. She was confident that she was one of life's chosen, and indeed seemed to be, and lived the part fully, while Bonnie was in her own eyes just a marginal sandwich-shop girl, the 'jeans-and-tee-shirts kind of girl' she had told Laura she was after their little window-shopping date at Bloomingdale's. Even though she didn't seem to pity herself, Laura felt a deep pang of sorrow for her.

"You are beautiful . . ." she purred again, now becoming more aggressive in her caresses, though certainly not initiating a new sexual episode. Instead, she thought, an 'affection' episode. "You are very lovely, inside and out." She rolled over onto Bonnie, straddling her thighs and now massaging her whole back, leaning down to rub own her naked breasts lightly across it, squeezing Bonnie's round, firm asscheeks with her fingers. "Believe me, I've been in bed with a lot of beautiful women, and you are right up there with them. You don't lose any points whatsoever for being a sandwich-shop girl."

Bonnie said nothing but smiled. Then she said, "That feels good. You have good hands."

Laura massaged her splendid back in silence. She kissed the nape of Bonnie's neck. Bonnie had short hair and it was easy to do. She then kissed the backs of her shoulders.

"You're gonna make me want to do it again if you keep that up," Bonnie warned softly, still smiling.

"Would you like me to see if I can find you a better job somewhere?" Laura heard herself asking, murmuring really, into the warm, sleek, deeply black skin of Bonnie's back.

Bonnie opened her eyes. "Your company got jobs?"

"Actually . . . no," Laura shook her head. "In fact, they're laying people off. But I have lots of contacts. I know somebody who works for the city."

Bonnie grinned, but her expression said that she knew better jobs existed but not for her. Laura pressed ahead.

"Can you type?"

"A little."

"You can answer a phone. Of course nowadays they don't need anybody to answer the phone. The machine does it."

Bonnie nodded and looked serene. "You stopped," she said, smiling lazily.

It was true. Laura had stopped rubbing her delicious back while she cogitated seriously on job opportunities for Bonnie. She resumed, leaning forward to kiss her between the shoulder blades. She let her lips trail along the smooth, hard flesh below one of them.

"How does that feel?" she whispered.

"Feels like my pussy be getting all oily wet," Bonnie giggled softly.

Laura ran her cheek along the same firm flesh she had been kissing. "Mmmm, I think I'm distracting you from our job search conversation."

"No kidding? You could help me get a job with the city?" Bonnie asked, twisting over and up in a way that made Laura disengage and move back to her side.

"I could try. Would you like that?"

Bonnie frowned. "Then I'd be obligated to you."

"You would not. I adore you."

"Wish you wouldn't say that all the time, Laura. I know you're 'married,' as you put it. You can't be adoring Bonnie Holland. You got somebody to adore already. I would be obligated to you." She smiled her simple, beaming smile. "Not that I'd mind. You ain't really bad to be obligated to. I could . . . you know . . . let you do things to me you want to do."

"You little tease," Laura pinched her thigh, which was difficult since Bonnie's thighs were well-muscled and hard.

Bonnie flirted. She was completely naked and swished her delectable breasts a little, knowing how that would catch Laura's attention. "And I could do things to you."

"You're doing them to me right now, you little tease. You don't play fair."

They embraced and fell back down on the bed, their naked breasts mashing happily together. Laura stroked Bonnie's back again with her fingertips.

"No kidding, you really could?" Bonnie asked.

"Do you want me to?"

"I guess so. I could sure use a little more money."

"You might have to work longer hours."

"Shit, I don't care. Better than just sitting around here, waiting for your 'wife' to go out of town."

This rang an alarm bell deep in Laura's mind, alerting her to an issue she meant to revisit at the first opportunity. Over-dependence on her attentions by any of her lovers was a red flag for Laura that she sought to lower as quickly and diplomatically as she could. Fortunately, in Bonnie's case, if she could get her a better job, with perhaps more upside potential than the sandwich shop one, then Bonnie's life would be fuller; and she would probably attract a wider selection of sexual partners, probably of both sexes, than she did now. Laura found her so compellingly simple, sweet, and sexy that she could not see how this could fail to be the case.

"You just need to branch out," Laura murmured, nuzzling her lovely black ear. "Find some other bed buddies . . . you know . . . like me."

"You mean other girls?" Bonnie grinned impishly. "You want to share me?"

Laura gave the appearance of thinking it over. "A lovely woman like you should not restrict herself to one already-taken partner. There's a lot of experience out there for you to grab."

"You mean lesbo experience."

"Not necessarily. Men have their place too."

"I had a few of them," Bonnie said glumly. "They ain't in the same league with you."

"Mmmmmm!" Laura grabbed her and squeezed her. "You really know how to make me hungry for you. Now turn back over. I want to make love to your beautiful bottom."

Bonnie smiled coyly again. "Long as you don't stick anything in it. One thing I like about you more than a man. You ain't always trying to stick something up my ass."

Little do you know, my pet, Laura thought, how I would like to ravish your beautiful posterior masterpiece. And yet, since you trust me not to, I'll have to continue to coax you along. You could go to heaven you haven't dreamed of yet. But it will still be there. She remembered how long it had taken even to get Bonnie this far.

"So . . . it's settled?" she asked, as she began to massage and rub and caress the phenomenal hard round up-jutting black moons of Bonnie's almost incredible ass. "I'm going to see if I can get you a better job?"

"Sounds like a plan," Bonnie said dreamily, again relapsing into sensual bliss as Laura's magical fingers dug into the hard flesh of her gorgeous rump. "That feels pretty good."

Someday you'll be like some other sweeties I know, begging me to fuck you in this marvelous ass, my sweet, Laura murmured to herself. But until then . . .

Since they had already fucked about an hour before this conversation, and had merely been lying and cooing together since then, Laura was certainly in no hurry to rush things. She loved taking the time she had never taken before to explore every inch of Bonnie's sweet body, kissing every inch of each round moon, then running her lips down to the crease where it met the top of Bonnie's thigh, and exploring that with her tongue. It was many long minutes before she even ventured into the deep, dark valley between them, rubbing it first gently with her forefinger, which sank a little deeper with each pass.

Bonnie said nothing, but Laura could notice her breathing subtly accelerating. She whimpered softly once. She was still smiling dreamily.

Of course, it wasn't every day that someone made love to your ass. In Bonnie's case, Laura reasoned, perhaps never. Men wanted to fuck it, true, but they probably never worshipped it as she was doing now.

"Ooooohhh!" Bonnie yelped softly, suddenly, as Laura's teeth sank gently into the firm round flesh of one bulging moon. Then she giggled, squirming a little. "You biting me too? You evil thing?"

"Grrrrr! I want to eat you alive," Laura growled playfully, nipping her other round cheek now the same way.

Bonnie laughed and squirmed some more, then stopped squirming and began softly moaning instead. "Shit . . . Laura, that feels good!"

"Mmmmm, you like that?"

Laura let her lips roam all over the beautiful, bulging black moons, baring her teeth now and then to take firm, smooth chunks of it between them, never biting hard but just enough to send a squirt of sensation through Bonnie's writhing body. Bonnie was beside herself with sensual pleasure, moaning softly now and gyrating her ass up into Laura's face, as if she couldn't get enough.

Without breaking the rhythm of her kisses and caresses, Laura reached up for a pillow and pulled it down, gently maneuvering Bonnie so that she could slip it under her hips, thus raising her ass up and exposing the festering, wet, dark pink slot of her lovely pussy just beneath the swelling black moons of her ass. Now Laura's voracious mouth could roam across the sweet lower regions of this marvelous girl with ease, and soon she was nipping and sucking the smooth ass flesh that was closer and closer to Bonnie's swollen, puckering wet vagina, and making Bonnie quiver and clench and whoop softly.

"Ooooooohhh! Oh . . . oh god . . . oh Laura . . . oh shit that feels good!"

"Oh, I want your pretty pussy," Laura cooed to her, now touching the warm wetness with two, three fingers, rubbing Bonnie's exposed clit, dipping lower with her head, trying to get her mouth on it too. "Scoot your ass up a little higher, honey," she coaxed Bonnie, who quickly complied, rising a little on her knees to make her pussy more available to Laura.

"Unnhhhh!" she gasped softly as Laura began to lick and suck her oozing cunt the same way she had been licking and sucking Bonnie's ass moons.

That meant a full-scale passion assault, a voracious slurping and sucking and mouth-mauling that was probably not what Bonnie had expected since it seemed to ratchet up her arousal to about triple the initial intensity. She began to twist and whimper and gyrate her pelvis, pushing her wet, inflamed cunt into Laura's mouth. Meanwhile, Laura was using the distraction of her busy mouth on Bonnie's aching pussy to further her other aims, getting two fingers into Bonnie's tight little ass crack, between the magnificent moons, and rubbing her fingertip against Bonnie's tight little anus.

She had no intention of invading it but wanted to give Bonnie the added hint of the fierce pleasure she could get if she desired it. And Bonnie responded by writing more violently and whimpering more hysterically.

"Ohhnnngggg . . . uuummmmnnnn . . . oh Laura . . . oh shit oh god . . . yes . . . yes . . . yes . . . unnhhhhhh!" she babbled incoherently, shimmying her terrific ass up into Laura's face and hand.

Oh honey, you are going to come, Laura said to herself, as if realizing they had got there sooner than she had expected to. You are going to come so hard. You are getting very hot. God, I love this beautiful ass. I just want to devour it.

"Oh Laura . . . oh yes . . . oh Laura . . . oh yes . . ." Bonnie chanted over and over into the sheet.

Laura heard herself grunting and snuffling softly with almost unconscionable passion as she hungrily devoured every sweet piece of Bonnie's beautiful black ass and pussy, rubbing Bonnie's hidden anus vigorously with the tip of her finger, using her other hand to massage Bonnie's swollen clit rapidly, bringing her up, up, closer, closer to the inevitable. Bonnie was a wreck, her lovely writhing body wound as tightly as Laura had ever seen her, straining and flexing, her sleek black flesh glimmering in the dim evening light.

"Unh . . . unh!" Bonnie gasped as she swirled her beautiful round ass back and up into Laura's face. "Oh! Oh . . . Laura . . ." she panted, looking over her shoulder, her face screwed up in a sweet agony of sexual pleasure. "Put . . . put your hand in me. Like before. Please."

Laura was caught a little by surprise, but not much. The very first time they had fucked, Laura almost by accident had ended up fisting Bonnie, who had experienced, apparently, the orgasm of her life. Ever since then Bonnie had become semi-addicted to this practice—which was not difficult, Laura knew, remembering Brenda and Mavis and a few others—and often tried to get Laura to do it again. From time to time

Laura complied. Who could deny her lover the kind of stirring, electrifying climaxes Bonnie had this way? And yet she often simply turned aside the request by a flood of hot passion so that it receded into the background until next time.

They had never done it from this position; Bonnie had always been on her back, where she could at the last moment reach down desperately and grab Laura's wrist, then literally rape herself wildly on it for the last few seconds before erupting in a shattering paroxysm of coming. That wouldn't work now, but there was otherwise nothing at all to prevent Laura from complying. She gazed into the festering, dark red, wet trench of Bonnie's gaping pussy, which glistened with juice as if beckoning her fingers, her hand, all slippery and gooey and in no need of more lubrication.

"Please!" Bonnie panted again, twitching her beautiful ass back into Laura's face. "Please, Laura . . . please!"

"Oh honey . . . oh honey!" Laura murmured over and over again, not knowing whether she was promising to deliver or trying to divert Bonnie's attention to a quick orgasm, which would have been no difficulty given her current state.

But Bonnie's feverish need got the better of her. Hell, if she wants it, she's got it, Laura thought. How can I deprive her?

She formed a little wedge with her fingers, and within seconds her whole hand was sunk in Bonnie's tight, wet pussy. She had always figured that one reason Bonnie loved this so much was that she had such a tight one, a very tight one, and that feeling it so thoroughly crammed with Laura's fist, was a sensation that could never be matched in any other way. It certainly was tight.

But it was also slippery wet and warm and squinchy, and Laura twisted her hand inside to give Bonnie the feelings she craved. At the same time, she completely mouth-mauled the girl's beautiful round bottom, sucking and biting her smooth black ass cheeks, and rubbing her anus vigorously with the forefinger of her free hand. Bonnie went absolutely wild.

This wasn't going to be any long, slow, smoldering build-up. She was nearly coming already. And her crazy, hysterical snorting and snuffling and grunting and flexing and squirming had an electrical effect on Laura, arousing in her the fierce lust required to bring Bonnie quickly over the top. Both of them were a wild, whimpering union of pumping, surging hot flesh.

"Unhhhh! Unngggmmnnnhhh! Ohnnnnggg! Umpphgghhh!" Bonnie groaned and panted, "nearly there, nearly there."

And Laura was equally vocal, though completely incoherent, she realized. She seemed to answer every one of Bonnie's grunts and moans with sympathetic grunts of her own. "Mmmmm . . . unnnnuummnnnnn . . . ungghhh! Ohnnnggg! Ummmmm!"

"Ooonngggg! Laura . . ." Bonnie panted wildly, her face contorted with fierce pleasure. "Harder! Do it . . . ooonnggggg . . . do it harder!"

Laura was amazed. Bonnie was such a sweet, shy, unassuming little thing, and yet in the heat of sex she could turn into a demon of lust, craving to be really pierced and skewered and roughed up by Laura's thrusting fist. She had done it before. She was sunk in a writhing seizure of extreme need and did not mind showing it, begging Laura to fuck her harder.

Ever willing, Laura picked up the pace, fucking Bonnie with her hand harder and faster, bringing more semi-hysterical whimpering from deep in Bonnie's lungs. Her hand inside Bonnie's pussy felt the contracting walls a split second before Bonnie herself even knew she was actually coming. But the arrival of the wrenching, rupturing orgasm overwhelmed both of them anyway.

"AWWWOONNGGGG!" Bonnie suddenly cried out, her luscious smooth body flipping and jerking spasmodically, but not enough to expel Laura's plunging hand.

Laura actually had a chunk of Bonnie's marvelous ass between her teeth just as the spasm hit, and of course it slipped out as Bonnie's ass cheek clenched into a hard ball. But her forefinger remained embedded deep in Bonnie's clenching asscrack, and she pressed her fingertip sharply against the girl's anus, rubbing it for maximum effect, and still slobbering hungrily over the gleaming black moons of Bonnie's ass as the wrenching shocks of Bonnie's orgasm ran their course.

It wasn't quick. Bonnie came unbelievably hard, whinnying into the sheet, her body quaking and straining, until the last excruciating drop of sweet pleasure had been squeezed out of her multiple orgasms. Even after that she lay face down, gasping and whimpering and twitching, with Laura's forearm still sticking up out of her impaled cunt. Laura wiggled her hand gently, as if about to withdraw it.

"Ahhhnnnn! Ahhnnnnn!" Bonnie gasped, wincing. "Please . . . not yet! Okay? Not yet."

She clenched her pussy around Laura's hand, pulsing it a few times, almost playfully, smiling with her eyes closed.

"You little minx," Laura teased, kissing her beautiful black buns tenderly. "You are enjoying this too much."

"What's a minx?" Bonnie continued smiling, still pinching Laura's hand now and then with her pussy.

"I don't know. A wanton woman, I guess." She nipped another hard round piece of flesh from Bonnie's lovely bare bottom. "Like you are."

"You know, men like it when you squeeze their cock with your pussy like this," Bonnie said, as if Laura, being a lesbian, needed to be informed of these things.

"I'll bet they like it when you do it," Laura murmured, unwilling to let her feasting on this marvelous ass be interrupted.

Now Bonnie opened her eyes. "Does that mean you don't like it?"

"I love it. But I'm getting a cramp," Laura confessed as she carefully extracted her wet hand from the girl's delightful tight honey pot. "If you ask me, I think you came enough to last you three weeks that time."

Bonnie nodded thoughtfully. "Guess it'll have to hold me. I tried it myself but my arm isn't long enough."

Laura smiled. "Now that is an image I will have no trouble recalling. The naked, infinitely desirable Bonnie lying here on this Murphy bed trying to get her own hand up her beautiful pussy. I think that'll be enough to get me off at any point during the day. Or night."

"You never need help doing that," Bonnie scoffed, sitting up. "Bet you have three or four girls you can call up if you need a quick little fuckie."

Laura hated this kind of conversation. She grabbed Bonnie and pulled her back down onto the sheet on her back, running one hand all over Bonnie's beautiful small high breasts, so firm and upswept, and kissing her cheek and then her high cheek bones. "Nobody with Choctaw Indian cheekbones like these, you marvelous creature," she said, tickling Bonnie under her arms and diverting her into a friendly tussle that ending in a romantic kiss, and ultimately in another sweet sexual clinch during which Laura received payment in full for her recent sweet labors.

LaVonda had got Laura's little 'fuck bunny,' as she called her, a job in the Redevelopment Agency, and Bonnie was quickly transformed from a simple sandwich shop girl into a crisply dressed and diligently hard-working office girl almost in a flash, before Laura's eyes. It was all very hard to believe.

First, Bonnie was no longer there when Laura dropped by the sandwich shop in the alley behind her building. This caused deep, alarming heart pangs. What have I done! Everybody will be fucking that lovely darling! She'll have no time for me!

Second, when she did meet Bonnie for lunch, she was happily taken aback by her altered appearance, almost entirely due to a change of wardrobe. No longer was Bonnie attired in a blue golf shirt and jeans. She wore a sharp, immaculate white shirt and tailored navy blue skirt, and a tasteful scarf; she looked amazingly fetching, but also office-perfect.

"Your friend LaVonda took me shopping," she confessed to Laura. "She said I had to be dressed a little better and she would help. Even loaned me the money."

Laura blushed slightly and looked away briefly to control her expression. "She's a wonderful person, isn't she? What a thing to do." And she meant it. She was astonished and pleased to hear of LaVonda's generosity.

They were sitting in a small café near City Hall. Bonnie took a sip of her lemonade.

"You and she . . . you know . . . do it. Right?" Her dark eyes flickered with what seemed to Laura a hint of jealousy as well as knowing amusement, as if to say: I know you do, no use denying it.

Laura smiled primly. It was impossible not to let her schoolmarmish nature surface at moments like this. "Of course we don't. We're . . . just friends."

Bonnie almost exploded with laughter, nearly spraying Laura with lemonade but covering her mouth at the last instant. Even so, droplets dribbled out between her fingers. Her eyes danced with wicked hilarity.

"You big liar!" she giggled. "You don't have to lie to me. I know you do it with her."

"Shhhh!" Laura cautioned, looking around. "I said that to protect her . . . not me. She works for the Mayor. Maybe she doesn't want it known."

"Oh." Bonnie calmed down and immediately banished the smile from her face. "Right. I forgot. You're probably right. Sorry."

Even though she was a little miffed with Bonnie for bringing it up, the whole episode, spraying lemonade and all, and Bonnie's laughter and cute accusations, made her fiercely desirable to Laura at that moment. Her lovely high cheekbones and the silky darkness of her skin emphasized by the crisp white cloth of her blouse made Laura's pussy tingle. God, I want her! I forgot how absolutely fetching she is.

"You need a ride home tonight?" Laura offered. "I could cruise by here and pick you up."

"You drive today? I thought you usually took BART."

"I had a meeting in Mountain View. Had to drive."

Bonnie's dark eyes twinkled again. "I know what you want."

Laura grinned at her. "Can you blame me? Look at yourself. The new Bonnie. I'm surprised the guys and gals aren't beating down your door for dates."

"Oh, I had a few showing some interest," Bonnie said airily, tossing her head with almost coquettish pride. "Mostly guys. Mostly looking at my ass. Like you do."

"I saw them," Laura said, truthfully. On their way to this café for lunch, she had seen several men turn to look at Bonnie's world class posterior with admiration and hunger.

She could also detect a flicker of sexual interest in Bonnie's eyes. Bonnie loved fucking with Laura, and loved Laura hungering after her phenomenal ass. "I guess I could use a ride," she said, with feigned disinterest, as if she would accept a ride only if she couldn't find anything better to do.

"I'll pick you up at five forty-five," Laura said decisively.

Bonnie frowned. "I get off at five. What am I supposed to do till then?"

Laura leaned across the small table and whispered, excited to bring her nose close enough to Bonnie's face so that she could inhale her thrilling fresh sexual odor. "Sit on the steps and think off all the things I'm going to do to your beautiful body."

Bonnie dissolved into giggles, so pleased she could clearly not contain it. Of all the girls Laura had wooed, Bonnie was, maybe along with Lila, the most likely to 'blush' at times like this. "God, I can really do that!" she laughed.

And when Laura pulled up in front of the Redevelopment Agency building promptly at five forty-five, Bonnie was indeed sitting on the steps with her arms hugging her shins, looking for all the world like a schoolgirl in her white sneakers, though without the plaid skirt, wearing the tailored, business-style one LaVonda had picked out for her instead. She does look young sometimes, Laura thought, waving and leaning across to open the passenger side door, knowing however that Bonnie was actually twenty-four. But she did look good enough to eat, at whatever age. My little fuck bunny, Laura thought happily. Am I ever going to fuck your cute bunny ears off.

Though Bonnie actually had pretty little well-shaped ears, very black, a little shiny, peaking out from beneath her short hair. Laura wanted to lean over and plunge her tongue into the closest one but didn't dare since they were in public.

Bonnie smiled a secretive, self-satisfied smile as Laura maneuvered in traffic toward the nearest Bay Bridge on-ramp. "Took your advice," she said. "I sat there and thought about all the things you gonna do to me."

Laura nearly frothed over with lust at the sound of these words. She gripped the steering wheel hard, but playfully. "Hold on, girl, you're going to make me lose control. Don't tell me any more until we get there. I'll faint with desire."

Bonnie giggled. "You are funny." After a minute, she added, "You make me feel good, Laura. Nobody ever wanted me as much as you do."

"Impossible," Laura said flatly. "You just didn't know it. Those high Choctaw cheekbones are enough to cause freeway pile ups. And that thing you're sitting on makes people whimper when you walk by."

Bonnie merely grinned with happiness and didn't reply. There was a long, slow traffic jam on the bottom deck of the Bay Bridge, and during the interminable crawl Laura had plenty of opportunity to look at Bonnie.

"You looking at me like I'm candy, Laura," Bonnie grinned.

"Or red meat to a hungry tiger," Laura teased, caressing Bonnie's shiny black kneecap with the fingertips of her right hand. "Tell me about your new job. To get my mind off it."

"What if I don't want to get your mind off it?" Bonnie flirted. "Maybe I like it when you want to screw me so bad. Like I say, you're worse than a man."

"I love your skin," Laura confessed, though it was nothing new to Bonnie. She caressed the smooth, glossy skin of Bonnie's thigh above her kneecap, just up to the point where the hem of Bonnie's skirt stopped her fingers.

"You sure like black girls, don't you," Bonnie said, but cheerfully, not reproachfully. "Why's that?"

"I like you," Laura said, a little forcefully, as she often did to turn aside this observation.

"And you like LaVonda. And your wife is black, ain't she?"

Laura nodded.

"That makes three of us."

"Just a roll of the dice," Laura said softly. "Lucky three. All three enchanting."

"You like their black skin too?"

Laura grinned and playfully pinched the flesh of her thigh, where she was caressing it. "You're getting personal."

Bonnie giggled. "We're gonna be in bed in about twenty minutes. How personal is that?"

Laura grimaced. "It may not be twenty minutes, the way this traffic is moving. Or not moving."

Bonnie was silent for another few minutes. Then she spoke softly, almost apologetically. "I don't care, you know."

"Don't care about what?"

"If you like other black chicks. I ain't ever been with any white chick but you, but you know how I like to look at our bodies together."

It was true. Bonnie had even pulled her large old combination bureau-dressing table that she had obviously got from the Salvation Army, with its tilting oval mirror, over within range of her Murphy bed so that she could watch them fucking while in progress. It was a very touching gesture, and Laura found that she liked watching their bodies coiled together too, out of the corner of her eye, when not too busy groaning and shuddering.

"What I mean is . . ." Bonnie began again, but Laura stopped her.

"I know what you mean," she grinned. "You mean I better watch out for the white girls instead of the black ones."

Bonnie giggled again.

"Now, tell me about your job. I want to know."

Bonnie gave a short narration of her daily duties. She liked her supervisor (male; fifties; white) but was wary of her head clerk (female; Hispanic; early forties and mean), and had already attracted some male attention from married and unmarried guys of several ethnic backgrounds. "One already asked me out," she said, proudly.

"And did you accept?"

"He's married. Got a big old gold ring on his hand. Thinks a little black pussy on the side would be fun."

God, he sounds like me! Laura suddenly thought, guiltily. The traffic finally picked up, and she realized they would get there after all.

"So . . . tell me what it's like to fuck with LaVonda," Bonnie said out of the blue, as they navigated the MacArthur Maze and headed for the Lake Merritt area where Bonnie's small apartment was located. "She's beautiful. She don't look any more like a lesbo than you do."

Laura pursed her lips. "You're one too, you know," she said. "You sleep with me."

Bonnie grinned widely. "Only we don't get no sleeping done." Then she grew solemn. "Sorry I said that. I don't know what they're supposed to look like."

They parked and went up to her apartment. "I'm still interested, though," Bonnie persisted. "I'd like to know what it's like. She's so different from me."

Now that they were not in public any longer, Laura could give in to her strongest impulses. She grabbed Bonnie and pulled her close and kissed her ravenously. Bonnie kissed back. She was panting mildly when Laura pulled away.

"That's okay, you can tell me later," she laughed. "I think we got other business first."

"I haven't touched you for so long . . . you set me on fire," Laura panted back, kissing Bonnie's shapely neck.

"Ooohhhh . . . that tickles," Bonnie gasped, squirming away. "Let me use the bathroom and then you can do all those things to me you were promising."

While Bonnie was in the bathroom, Laura, who had some practice from previous occasions, let down the Murphy bed, and pulled back the bedcovers, exposing the sheet. She caught her own eye in Bonnie's tilting oval mirror, which was positioned precisely to pick up activities on the bed. You revolting little roué, she told herself. Despoiling this poor sweet girl's virtue.

When Bonnie emerged from the bathroom, she was carrying her blouse and skirt, wearing only her underwear: simple white bra, simple white cotton underpants. She wiggled her breathtaking bottom at Laura. "This what you were waiting for?"

Laura was already unbuttoning and unzipping her own clothes as she watched Bonnie cross the room. Her mind flitted back to the days when she had bought her lunchtime sandwiches from this marvelous girl, feeling her heart flutter and her pussy pulse as Bonnie's fingertips lingered in her palm while making change, thinking it was a gesture meant only for her, Laura, until she gulped to see Bonnie doing it with everyone. It was not a sexual sign after all, just a byproduct of Bonnie's extraordinary sweet nature and friendliness.

"God, I wanted you from the start," she confessed, now down to her underwear too. "You are a vision."

Bonnie deposited her clothes on a chair and came over to Laura. "You just horny, that's all."

They embraced by the bed, Laura peeking over Bonnie's shoulder at their image in the oval mirror, watching her pale hands running all over Bonnie's dark, smooth back, impeded only by the thin straps of Bonnie's bra. "I am so going to fuck you and make you scream with joy," she murmured, finally getting the chance to slither her tongue deep into Bonnie's enchanting black ear. "I want to eat you alive."

Bonnie shivered and laughed. Being a little shorter than Laura, she tilted her face up and pulled Laura's face down to it with one hand behind Laura's head, kissing her ardently. "You can fuck me as much as you want," she said into Laura's teeth.

Laura kissed her back, a searing, scorching kiss, plunging both hands under the elastic band of Bonnie's underpants at the same time and clutching the firm round balls of her incredible ass. "I want to fuck you all night," she breathed into Bonnie's ear.

Again Bonnie giggled. "People always say they want to do that," she pulled Laura closer to the bed. "Nobody can do it all night. We'll get pretty tired first."

Laura got Bonnie's bra unclasped and pulled it off, cupping and squeezing the girl's marvelous springy young breasts. "Not me. I can keep going forever with someone like you. You make me so horny. I want to . . ."

Bonnie forced Laura around so that she too could unclasp Laura's bra. "I know what you want to do. You told me. You want to eat me alive."

Laura snarled and bit her smooth neck lightly, pinching her incredible bottom at the same time. "Right. I do. And I'm going to. Take these off."

She pulled Bonnie's panties down around her knees. Now both laughing, they tumbled happily onto the bed and helped each other get completely naked. Then they embraced for a long, sensual kiss, suppressing the sexual urgency they both felt in favor of a lengthy, slow, passionate communion, luxuriating in the feel of their warm naked bodies squirming together.

"Mmmm, that's what I like about you, Laura," Bonnie finally murmured. "You like to fuck, but you ain't in no hurry. Plenty of time to kiss and rub. That's what I like, kissing and rubbing."

"Me too," Laura murmured back, rubbing her body aggressively against Bonnie's. "And sucking. Don't forget sucking. Laura loves sucking."

She dropped her mouth to Bonnie's breasts, and Bonnie watched. "Nobody ever sucked like you do," she agreed.

One of the most moving and erotic things Bonnie did—and she had done it from the start—was to caress Laura's hair, her forehead, her temples, lightly, affectionately, with the fingers of one hand while Laura was ardently sucking her nipples, or even while Laura was licking her pussy or even fist-fucking her, which Bonnie craved above all things. No matter how aroused she was becoming, she could not prevent these sweet, loving caresses from emerging, and Laura found them extremely touching.

Now was no different. Laura sucked one of Bonnie's firm little breasts with extravagant care and tenderness and wet-lipped passion, and Bonnie's fingertips danced lovingly over Laura's hair, then her forehead.

"Ohhhhhhh!" Bonnie sighed. "Yes. Laura . . . you suck so good. Makes me hot."

Laura, still sucking happily, glanced briefly to the side and saw their reflection in the mirror, a stunning tableau of pale and dark skin and curves and gleaming flesh and lips and flashing eyes. Bonnie saw her looking, and their eyes met in the mirror.

"You like to watch too," Bonnie smiled.

"We're beautiful," Laura said, pausing only briefly before trying to inhale Bonnie's other breast.

Bonnie caressed Laura's shoulders, and her neck, and her cheek, with those soft fingertips. "I love it when you do that," Laura whispered.

"This?"

"Yes. I love it."

Bonnie smiled, bemused. "I didn't even know I was doing it. You make me feel good."

Laura paused, still holding Bonnie's enchanting saliva-wet breasts cradled in both hands. She looked up at Bonnie. "Okay . . . now you get to choose how you want me to do you. Let's see. We can pussy fuck. I can lick you to heaven, and suck your pretty little clittie. I could—"

Bonnie interrupted her. "You know what I want."

Laura smiled. "Or . . . we could do that."

Bonnie nodded slowly. "I can think of something else, though," she said, almost shyly, as if it were too audacious to bring this up.

"What?"

"You know"—she was almost blushing, though dark as coal, and could not look Laura directly in the eye—"last time when we did that? And you were rubbing my little booty hole with your finger when I was coming?"

Laura nodded. "You really exploded."

Bonnie would still not look her in the eye. "I think . . ."

"You want me to do that again?"

Bonnie nodded slowly. "And . . ."

"Stick it in?"

Bonnie shrugged. Her marvelous round breasts jiggled in Laura's cradling hands. She now looked Laura directly in the eye. "I think I could do it. I mean, take it. I been thinking about it over and over. How it might make me come so hard I . . ."

"So hard you almost can't stand it?" Laura added, now squeezing the marvelous round balls with her fingers, eager to get her hungry mouth on them again.

Bonnie smiled and giggled again, shyly. "I can try to stand it."

"Mmmmm, I'll only do it if you let me suck these again for about an hour," Laura said, dropping her mouth to one bulging black nipple, laving it with her tongue.

Bonnie said nothing but began to breathe a little harder as she watched Laura devouring her breast. "I don't know if I can wait an hour," she finally said, panting harder. "You're making me want it bad."

Laura held Bonnie's wet, bulbous nipple between her lips and looked up at her. "Me too," she said, without letting it go.

With Laura still sucking her breast, Bonnie stretched out sensually on her back, parting her thighs and in effect presenting her entire body to Laura. And what a body it was. Laura was capable of ascending to rhapsodies of sexual desire just in contemplation of it. Bonnie was not voluptuous, like LaVonda for example, but built more on athletic lines. Except for her firm, high, opulent bottom, she was lean and well-toned and sleek and firm and very dark, a feast for the lips, as Laura, who explored her flesh hungrily each time they were together, well knew.

She wanted to continue her slow, sensual feast right now, but Bonnie was getting overheated. She was a freak for fist-fucking—shades of that darling Mavis! Laura thought—and would not settle for slower, gentler, more simmering methods until she got her first wrenching, groaning, debilitating orgasm out of the way. And this time she wanted

Laura to finger her ass too, the first time she had asked, which would doubtless send her to the moon.

"Are you sure?" Laura cooed to her as she reluctantly let her mouth and fingers leave Bonnie's hard wet nipples and descend toward the delicious lower regions of her body. "You sure you want it?"

Bonnie lifted her head long enough from the mattress to glower down at Laura, as if she had already made it perfectly clear. "I want it."

Laura smiled at her. "I have to get my handbag."

In a trice Laura was off the Murphy bed, swooping and dipping over to the kitchen chair where she had dropped her purse, quickly extracting the small bottle of oil she always kept in it. Mercifully Bonnie's tiny one-room apartment ensured that things could not be very far apart, and she was back on the bed before half a minute had elapsed. Bonnie was looking at her as if some curious medical procedure was about to occur.

"What are you doing?"

Laura held up the little bottle. "Oil, my pet. Makes it easier."

"Oh."

Laura loved Bonnie's sleek naked body, and this was a task, making love to these two portals she was about to invade with maximum ardor, that she was very willing to prolong. Bonnie, patient and curious as ever, yielded her body completely to Laura's loving ministrations, biting her full lower lip as Laura's greased finger slid for the first time up into her ass, her black eyes watering a little.

"Unhhhhh!" she gasped softly. "Oh!"

"Does that feel good?"

An unexpected grin—unanticipated by either one of them—spread over Bonnie's face. "You know . . . it does . . . kind of."

Laura slowly swiveled her finger, probing gently. But she could not keep her eyes off Bonnie's swollen pussy, a feast she could barely keep herself from falling on with crazy lust. It was a beautiful little pussy, a tight little slot of now-puffy black cunt lips enclosing a shiny dark pink wet feast of oozing inner pussy meat, the whole delicious slit surrounded by a fringe of coal-black crotch hair, which Laura spread aside with the fingers of her free hand to make everything available to her probing tongue.

"Unhhh! Anngghh!" Bonnie gasped, her hips quivering a little as she accustomed herself to Laura's invading mouth, which she had apparently not expected, at least not so soon. "Ohhhhhhh! Oh . . . Laura . . . that feels good!"

Laura, as she settled into seriously making love to Bonnie's pussy with her mouth and fucking her sweet little virgin asshole with her greased finger, wondered if they would actually ever get to the thing Bonnie wanted most, at least this first time around. True, Bonnie adored being fist-fucked, and would never let an opportunity like this one go by without demanding it, and yet at the moment she was quickly losing control, a state Laura did everything to encourage.

You can come this way, darling, you can come. And it will be so good, I guarantee it. Just let me take you there. We can do the other later on, I promise. Just give in to it now, okay? Just relax and let this wonderful orgasm come to you, okay?

"Oh shit that feels good!" Bonnie panted, now gyrating her pelvis, pushing her ass down on Laura's slowly thrusting hand, and her pussy up into Laura's devouring mouth.

"Mmmm . . . it's going to feel even better," Laura panted, cranking up the heat, fucking her faster, sucking her harder, taking

Bonnie's thickening little clit between her lips and tormenting it with hungry passion.

"Oh! Oh!" Bonnie gasped, her eyes rolling up. With one hand she grabbed her jiggling breasts and squeezed them roughly, first one, then the other, pinching her black shiny nipples. "Unhhhh! Oh!"

By now Laura knew they were going for the finish line, whether Bonnie knew it yet or not. Yes, honey, yes! Go for it! Feel it coming!

"Annhhh . . . ohhnnggg . . ." Bonnie twisted and groaned.

This went on for another minute or more. Laura took her whole clit, hood and all, into her mouth, lashing it with her tongue and sucking insistently. Her forefinger probed and swiveled inside Bonnie's clenching rectum, and she knew it was here, the fierce spasm they were awaiting, it was welling up inside Bonnie's flexing, straining body, her sleek flesh tightening in a killing paroxysm of sexual rapture. And then it arrived, and Bonnie exploded.

"AUUNGGGHHHH!" she roared, her strong young body jackknifing violently up off the Murphy bed, her breasts shimmying and her black thighs gleaming and flexing.

Laura out of the corner of her eye caught their reflection in the tilted oval mirror Bonnie had set up just for this moment, and she was almost paralyzed by the beauty not only of their blended naked bodies but of Bonnie's seizure of ecstasy. Unfortunately, Bonnie was in no position to see it herself, having been propelled into orgasmic paradise by the force of her shattering climax. Her eyes were closed, her lovely face still contorted by the sharp force of her pleasure, her body only now slackening as the spasms waned.

But Laura could enjoy it all, and she did, soon realizing that she was looking at Bonnie's lovely dark body in the mirror more than directly. As Bonnie slowly drifted back from the crushing swoon of her ecstasy, her eyes fluttered open and she saw Laura looking at them in the mirror. She smiled lazily. Laura turned her face back.

"You came hard."

Bonnie nodded. She looked down at her crotch, where Laura's hand was still stuck, Laura's forefinger still embedded in her ass. "The magic finger," she grinned.

Laura smiled back, removing it slowly, wiping it clean on the edge of the sheet. "I guess so. Certainly worked for you."

Bonnie, still on her back, drew Laura down into a lazy embrace. She kissed Laura long and slow. "You are turning me into a sex maniac."

"Really?"

Again Bonnie nodded slowly. "My mama used to say that when I was a teenager. Crazy about boys. 'They sex maniacs, girl. They'll corrupt you. They'll deliver you right up to the devil. Sex is for making babies, that's all. You keep those nasty maniacs away from that young pussy, you hear?' That's what she said."

"Good thing she's never met me, I guess," Laura said, kissing her back.

"She would freak if she knew I'm a lesbian. I think in her mind that would be even worse than a maniac. She would just have a heart attack and die if she could see us right now."

Laura nuzzled her neck. "Maybe because we're so beautiful together."

Again they both admired their coiled-together bodies in the mirror. "I like looking at us," Bonnie murmured after a while. She spread her very black hand over the pale, creamy expanse of Laura's naked back. "See?"

"It was a great idea, pulling the mirror over here."

"Here . . . move over here . . . like this . . ." Bonnie prompted, maneuvering Laura's body on the bed. Laura complied. "I'm going to eat your pretty pink pussy and make you come while I watch you in the mirror," Bonnie said, with ill-concealed pleasure.

But Laura had already clamped her legs on one of Bonnie's hard, sleek, black thighs and pushed her creaming, oozing pussy down on it, excited and reminded both of the sight seconds ago when she had seen Bonnie's glossy thighs flexing in the mirror as Bonnie came, and also of the time a few weeks back when she had persuaded LaVonda to fuck her that way, in the old 'Brandi' way, fucking Laura's pussy with her hard, muscular thigh. Oh god, I am becoming a fanatic, she thought. A maniac in my own way. I want her to do it!

"Can we do that later?" she murmured in Bonnie's ear. "I . . . have a little request."

Bonnie could be so loving at tender moments like this that it was very touching. She caressed Laura's temple with her fingertips, brushing away a few strands of hair. "What is it?" she asked softly, eyes wide.

"I want to just keep doing this," Laura replied, pushing her wet cunt into the hard muscle of Bonnie's smooth thigh.

Bonnie's mouth cracked open in a wide grin. "You mean you can get off this way?"

"I sure can. I'm almost there already. If you kiss me again, I'll probably come."

Bonnie gave her another one of those exquisitely tender caresses she seemed to specialize in, this time with the fingertips of her other hand across Laura's cheek. "I love to watch you come, too," she confessed softly. "I love to see the look on your face."

She clenched the thigh muscle that was pressed tightly against Laura's aching pussy. Laura's eyes rolled up. "Unhhhhh! Oh yes . . . just like that!"

"Mmmm, guess we better ride this horse in the direction it's going," Bonnie murmured softly, kissing Laura's cheek, then her mouth, all the while increasing the pressure of her thigh muscle in the warm, wet groove of Laura's splayed pussy. "If you're gonna come, we better get on with it."

They struggled gently for a few seconds to find the right rhythm and position—whether Laura should be on her back, or whether Bonnie should with Laura riding hard on top—and finally ended up in the latter. Unlike Brandi or LaVonda, Bonnie just did not have the temperament to give Laura the quick, aggressive, even briefly brutal plowing she felt she needed, but she knew she could achieve it herself if she were on top.

"Yes . . ." she panted, clamping Bonnie's thigh with both of her own, enjoying the feel of her naked breasts mashing down into Bonnie's, feeling the hard nubs of Bonnie's nipples jabbing her own, kissing her roughly, still panting, now grunting softly a little as she pushed her slippery cunt up and down on the large, hard, smooth muscle of Bonnie's wonderful thigh. "Yes . . . unhhhh . . . like that . . . ohhnnn . . . oh yes oh yes! Oh Bonnie!"

"Laura, I think you're gonna pop," Bonnie smiled, panting a little too from the effort of pushing her leg up into Laura's crotch, still letting her fingertips lightly caress Laura's arms and shoulders as Laura pumped her way toward paradise.

"Oh god yes I am!" Laura gasped. "Unnnggghhh! Ungghh! Ohhmmggnniee!"

She came in a hot, quick fury, feeling the stabbing flames of her orgasm down to the soles of her feet as her body quaked and shuddered on top of Bonnie's, her cries slowly dying into soft, keening sighs as she slumped forward, panting in Bonnie's ear.

"Oh god, you are a heavenly girl!" she panted to Bonnie, overcome once more by the tenderness of Bonnie's fingers caressing her forehead, and Bonnie's lips on her neck.

"I ain't heavenly," Bonnie giggled softly. "I just like fucking with Laura. We take each other to heaven, right?"

Laura nodded groggily, finally lifting her head, then pushing her body up so that her breasts were no longer mashing into Bonnie's. "Heaven," she croaked.

"Never knew you could come that way," Bonnie said. "I guess it figures, though. I think I could too. You just jam yourself down on me that way, and then the bombs go off, right? I think I'll have to try it."

Laura, now recovering her breath, gave a burping little laugh. "I guess you will."

But Bonnie became kittenish. She pulled Laura close again and slithered her tongue into Laura's ear. "But first . . . you know what I want."

"I know what you want, you little pervert." She ran her hands down Bonnie's lovely naked back to her hard, high buns and squeezed them sharply. "Imagine what your mother would think to overhear you," she teased. "A lesbian who likes to be fist-fucked. Shame!"

Bonnie laughed her musical, throaty laughter, throwing her head back a little, revealing her enchanting black throat, which Laura kissed hungrily. "Tell you one thing," she said through her laughter. "If Laura did it to Mama, Mama would like it too."

"Ooooohhhh," Laura tickled her ribs, tussling with her, luxuriating in the feel of Bonnie's taut, smooth young flesh rubbing her own. "I'll bet your mama is good-looking too, when you look at how gorgeous you are. Does she have these high marvelous cheekbones too? Maybe she'd like a little Laura-lovin'. Maybe I could turn her."

"Are you kidding? The Lord will strike us both dead if we keep talking like that."

Bonnie was only half-joking. She grew serious. She rubbed her naked body against Laura's more seriously too, looking in the oval mirror at their entangled pale and dark flesh. "Look at us. You getting me hot again. I'm forgetting all about my mama. She can go watch Dr. Phil or something and leave me to my Laura."

She grabbed Laura's hand, the one she knew would be fisting her to heaven in just a few minutes, and peppered it with kisses.

"Why do you like it so much?" Laura murmured to her after a few minutes of kissing and rubbing and raising the heat in their bodies about fifty degrees. She pretty much knew the answer, she thought, but would love hearing Bonnie tell it.

"I never had an orgasm in my life like I had the first time you did it to me," Bonnie confessed shyly. "And," she beamed, "every time since. It just makes me come so hard."

Laura nibbled her earlobe. "I thought you might say that," she whispered. "Sometimes you go wild."

"Are you kidding? I go wild every time."

"I love it when you grab my arm and sort of jam your pussy down on my wrist."

She saw Bonnie's dark eyes go momentarily glassy as she heard the words coming out of Laura's mouth. "You love it? Guess how much I love it."

Laura kissed her and clutched her body hard. "God, you are making me so horny just talking about it."

"Me too. Here, feel." She drew Laura's hand down to her crotch, which was sopping wet with warm pussy juice. "I'm ready."

"You sure are," Laura smiled, frightfully aroused herself. "Lie back, my darling. Auntie Laura is about to send you to the ninth circle of heaven."

Bonnie smiled, almost coyly. "Love it when you talk dirty to me, too. 'I want to fuck you, Bonnie, baby,' and 'I just love your sweet pussy, Bonnie, baby' and stuff like that."

"Mmmmm," Laura pushed her face into Bonnie's smooth neck, kissing and sucking it playfully, squeezing one of the girl's luscious firm breasts in her hand. "Like 'Let me fist fuck your beautiful black pussy, Bonnie, baby?' Like that?"

Bonnie nodded, suddenly squirming under Laura's hand, as if the words themselves were nearly too hot to bear. "Like that. You gonna do it?"

Laura kissed the breast she was holding in one hand, then sucked Bonnie's large, soft black nipple deep into her mouth.

"Ohhhhnnnmmmm!" Bonnie moaned, writhing a little.

"I am," Laura murmured, her mouth descending down Bonnie's delicious naked body. "I am."

She saw Bonnie glancing up at the mirror, as if she didn't want to miss watching them, their reflection, even as she was being overwhelmed by surging sexual feelings. Laura smiled up at her. "You naughty thing. Looking."

"I like looking," Bonnie smiled back.

By now Laura was working two, then three fingers, finally four, then her thumb, then the whole wedge, into Bonnie's wet pussy, pushing, feeling it opening, yielding, letting her hand inside. They had done this often—every time! Laura realized—and were used to the slow, sensual rhythm of penetration, and the accompanying physical excitement and emotional crescendo. There was something very intimate about fist-fucking, something that made you melt in awe and deep churning passion and molten sensuality, and often as they did it they were groping clumsily, desperately for each other, kissing, mewling and frantic with crazy lust and need.

Bonnie was no longer looking, at least not at the mirror. Instead she was gazing down at Laura's arm protruding from her engorged cunt, her wet black cunt lips clinging to Laura's wrist. Laura's small, clumped hand was completely inside her pussy, and Bonnie was semi-swooning in the preliminary stages of what Laura knew would become a shattering climax.

"Ohhhnnnn! Annngghhhhh!" she moaned, twisting and gyrating her hips, grinding her tight, warm, slippery pussy into Laura's hand. "Oh yes Laura oh yes yesssssss!"

Laura leaned closer, kissing her smooth cheek, her forehead. "Open your eyes . . . look . . . look at me fisting your beautiful black pussy, Bonnie . . ."

"Oh god!" Bonnie couldn't open her eyes. They were rolling up, her eyelids fluttering wildly.

"Oh, I love to fuck you," Laura chanted softly to her, as Bonnie had asked her to do. "And to make you come. I love to make you come so hard you nearly pass out. I love to fist fuck your beautiful pussy. Is it good? Is it good, darling?"

With a desperate upward lunge, Bonnie looped one arm around Laura's neck and brought Laura's mouth down on hers, so hard that their teeth clanked painfully. Their tongues coiled and stabbed together. Bonnie was panting feverishly as they kissed, jamming her impaled pussy down on Laura's hand, grinding, mewling and whooping softly, gyrating her hips, churning. She was clearly out of control, shooting the moon, and Laura knew her climax could not be far off. Both had forgotten the mirror in the frenzy of this moment.

"Unh! Unh! Unh! Onnnhhgggnnn! Ummnngg! Ummnngghh!" Bonnie gasped and panted, twisting and surging, finally dropping her hand between them, as she often did, to grab Laura's forearm and jam her pussy down onto Laura's wrist.

Usually she came shortly after this, but now it was as if she could not get enough of this feeling and wanted to prolong it, extend it as far as it would go before the sheer force of her inevitable orgasm overtook her. They were locked in this fierce but awkward embrace, Bonnie rocking, Laura holding steady, cooing to her, kissing her, Bonnie's sharp crotch thrusts becoming more and more insistent, even violent.

"Oh! Oh!"

"Yes, honey, yes!" Laura kissed her neck, her cheek, her forehead, peppering her face with passionate kisses, giving short forward thrusts with her fist to meet Bonnie's violent churning and pumping. "Yes . . . oh yes . . ."

"Ungghhh! Oh shit! Ungghhh! Oh . . . Laura . . . ungghhhh! Oh!"

Now, for the first time Laura could remember, Bonnie dropped her other hand too and grabbed Laura's forearm with it, so that she was holding Laura's arm with both hands. She jammed her pussy down on Laura's wrist as strongly as she could, almost wailing and shrieking with the crazy force of her arriving orgasm.

"Annngghiiiieeeeee!" she wailed, her body flipping and jackknifing as the wrenching spasms took her. "Annngghiiiieeeee! Ummnngghiiieeee!"

Laura could only hold on, awestruck by the force of Bonnie's climax, which seemed stronger than any she could recall the girl having in their months together. Bonnie surged and flexed, then seemed to dissolve back into the sheets, her body going slack and her facial contortions relaxing, as she nearly blacked out from the sheer power of her climax. Laura had seen it before now and then, and many times, of course, with both Makeeda and Jonelle, these swooning types of orgasms that seemed to be almost life-threatening, though she had never had one quite so obliterating herself. And Bonnie had never had one until now.

And here I am with my hand up this poor swooning girl's sweet tight pussy while she tries to regain consciousness, Laura thought, with a little mordant twist, smiling at herself wryly in the mirror. Her hand could still feel the waning contractions of Bonnie's cunt. She could not take her eyes off Bonnie's lovely slackened naked body and her own wrist protruding from Bonnie's crotch, an obscene but thrillingly sexual sight in the same instant, and not without its perverse beauty. I would love to have a photo of this to look at now and then, she smiled at herself even more wryly.

Bonnie now began to stir. Laura started slowly to withdraw her hand, but Bonnie clamped her delicious, sleek black thighs on it. "Don't you dare," she croaked in a soft, hoarse voice, her eyes blinking open. "I love it."

"Evidently you do," Laura whispered, leaning down again to kiss her, a long, romantic kiss this time. "I thought you might just tear it off and keep it."

"Would if I could," Bonnie smiled lazily, finally unclamping her thighs and letting Laura carefully extract the small, skilled hand that had caused her such exquisite pleasure.

Laura cleaned off her hand and they embraced full-length, stretching out so that every inch of their bodies could touch, their toes curling and twisting together, their open mouths locked together. They looked at themselves in the mirror, luxuriantly caressing and kissing. "We are a picture," Laura said softly.

Bonnie smiled and nodded. "I know I've said this before . . . but I never came that hard in my life."

Laura laughed and nodded. "You had me worried for a few minutes."

"Does LaVonda come like that when you do it with her?"

Laura had to choose between being irritated at Bonnie's tasteless prying or indulgent of her artless curiosity. She chose the latter, shaking her head. "One other," she said softly. "Maybe two. My sweetie does . . . sometimes."

Bonnie beamed. "Maybe that means I'm a little like her, at least."

"A little. You sure came hard."

"I know," Bonnie blinked. "I can still feel it. Almost. Like . . . cobwebs. Know what I mean?"

"I wish. I don't think I've ever had an orgasm like that."

Bonnie grew more aggressive with her caresses. "We can try. Maybe if I fist you, too."

Laura nuzzled her smooth black neck, now oily with a thin film of sweat inspired by their energetic fucking of the past hour. "Why don't we have something to eat first? I'm starved. Pour me a little vodka and teach me how to make that slum gullion of yours that I love so much."

Bonnie became positively girlish. She popped out of bed. "You know I got a new bottle? And some tonic water too? Just to be prepared. I know what Laura likes."

Laura could not take her eyes off her. Bonnie was still gloriously naked, moving about the apartment as if all that delicious firm black flesh was not driving Laura's lust meter up to the stratosphere again. "Put on something," Laura said. "A robe. A tee shirt. I can't bear watching your beautiful body."

From across the room Bonnie shot her a flirtatious smile. "Maybe I just get you your little drinkee and we wait till later for the slum gullion."

Laura laughed, still drinking up Bonnie eagerly with her eyes. "Better hurry or I might even want to skip the drinkee."

To be continued...

Miranda Mars

The Girl of My Girl

BONNIE CHRONICLES 3

Erotic Lesbian Romance

Laura realized she had a sharp desire to see Bonnie, whom she had not seen for weeks due to a variety of circumstances. Now that Bonnie was working at the job LaVonda had procured for her with the city, she was not only less dependent on Laura but not as close, either; seeing her was not as easy as popping down to the sandwich shop in the alley, where Laura had first met her. If she didn't stay in touch, Laura had to take the extra step to track her down. She did not have Bonnie's cell phone number, which was something she intended speedily to correct.

With this in mind, on a day when she had to drive to work due to meetings outside the office, she decided to cruise by the Redevelopment Agency, where Bonnie worked, a little after five, when she knew Bonnie would be getting off. To her great surprise, she even managed to snag a parking space about a third of a way down the block. She fed the meter and waited, thinking to surprise Bonnie, to give her a ride home, and then go up to Bonnie's little studio apartment and fuck the dear girl for about three hours. *God, I could really get into that*, she realized, squirming in her seat. It had been two days since her tryst with Shelley, and Makeeda was not due home until the end of the week.

You, my dear, she told herself, *are a lust-drenched sex maniac.* Poor Bonnie! The moment she sees you, she probably thinks: *Oh god, that sex fiend Laura wants to fuck me again.*

Imagine her shock when she saw Bonnie emerge from the RDA building with a blonde girl, laughing and joking and walking together in the direction of the Civic Center BART station. The girl was about the same height as Bonnie but huskier, with a butch haircut. *Lesbo*, Laura thought, gnawing her lower lip. *Trying to poach my sweetie. What am I going to do?*

She promptly started up her car and pulled out to follow them, but traffic held her up, naturally, and by the time she got free she slowly drove by the BART station in time to see the blonde butch girl waving goodbye as Bonnie started down the stairs. Honking was useless.

Anyway, she didn't want to make a spectacle, as if she had been shadowing them.

She drove to Bonnie's apartment in Oakland and waited a decent interval before going up. It was embarrassing. Now more than ever she began feeling that Bonnie would think: *oh, it's that damn Laura again, wanting to fuck me. Never see her around here unless she got black pussy on the brain.* It did seem an awfully lot like that.

But Bonnie was not at home. Laura knew that the BART train would have made it there long before she did, and so Bonnie must've stopped off on the way, perhaps for a little grocery shopping. She waited. She felt silly hanging around near Bonnie's door in the corridor of the small apartment house, so she went downstairs and waited by the curb. Soon Bonnie appeared, carrying a brown supermarket bag.

"Laura!" she smiled. She seemed genuinely happy to see Laura.

For her part, Laura could not take her eyes off Bonnie, who even at the end of a day's work looked fresh and delicious in her office garb and white sneakers. *I have held this darling in my arms and made her pant, and whinny through her beautiful orgasms*, she realized. Sometimes it was hard to believe it. She is so sweet and natural and shy and pretty, and has those devastating high cheekbones. No wonder Butch Blondie wants to do the same thing.

"I . . . went by your work to offer you a ride," Laura said, blurting it out foolishly. "Guess I missed you . . . but I really wanted to see you . . . so I came here."

Bonnie's dark eyes almost twinkled. "Bet I know why."

"Oh god, caught out again," Laura spoofed herself.

"You wanted some of my good home cooking," Bonnie smiled, looking down at the grocery bag she was holding against her marvelous jutting young breasts, which Laura had sucked so hungrily on so many occasions, before melting down totally in orgasms divine of her own.

Laura grinned. "That's it. You mind reader."

"Onliest trouble is, somebody else is coming too." Bonnie gave her a troubled, ambiguous look. "Friend from work."

Uh oh. Laura felt her spirits, seconds ago skyrocketing in the anticipated thrill of hot fucking with this delicious girl, suddenly plummet. She could not even control her reaction. "Don't tell me. Blonde? Short haircut?"

Bonnie looked quizzical. "How'd you know?"

"I saw her with you as you were entering the BART station. You were waving goodbye."

"She's going home to get her car. She lives in the city and has to get back after . . . dinner. Don't like riding BART at night." Bonnie paused uncomfortably.

Did this mean they were already doing it, already a couple, had already fucked and writhed and panted and fucked and . . . ? Laura thought in a heated, jealous frenzy. Or were they planning to do it tonight for the first time, after 'dinner'?

She also hated herself for this petty jealous streak, which for years now she had successfully managed to suppress. After all, she had encouraged Bonnie to make friends at her new job, male or female, to fill her life (and her bed) without depending on Laura to fill it. *Be careful what you wish for*, she told herself. Somebody else will hold her tonight. Somebody else will hear those sweet little whimpers. Somebody else will shove her brutal fist up into that beautiful tight pussy (Bonnie's sex act of choice; who would guess, looking at this sweet, innocent darling in her white tennies and her crisp blouse and simple skirt, that she loved being fist-fucked into screaming paroxysms of ecstasy?). Oh god.

Laura gulped, visibly shaken but trying to hide it from Bonnie. I must not let her know that I'm upset by it, she thought. She looked down at the sidewalk and shuffled her feet. "Well . . . it was just a thought. I better get going." She smiled, falsely bright. "So you can get up there and start cooking." She pulled away, desperately wanting Bonnie to call her back.

Bonnie did not. "Why don't you come by tomorrow night?"

Laura continued to smile tightly. "Sure. Maybe I'll do that."

"Really." Bonnie flooded her with a warm smile. "Promise?"

"I promise."

Laura felt like her face might be in danger of breaking into pieces from this tight smile as she climbed back behind the wheel of her car. *I am so furious and sad that I . . . what? I can't make love to her tonight? I am so selfish. Bonnie has a life. She can spread her darling joy anywhere, and I encouraged her to do it! Tonight Butch Blondie is the lucky girl, not me. Poor Laura. Grow up!*

Time passed. As it inevitably did. Work intervened. Arthell intervened. The time had come to give Bonnie another try, pretending nothing awkward had happened between them, and that Laura's feelings were not bruised by having been given the brush off. An exhausting evening in Arthell's parents' bed, fucking the dear girl to oblivion and back to the point where neither of them could even summon the energy to get dressed, had been enough to assuage Laura's feelings of rejection for a while. She did not, as promised, contact Bonnie the next day, hoping back deep in her mind somewhere that Bonnie herself would feel vaguely wounded, and that somehow would even things up between them. Instead, she let two weeks elapse before calling her. During this period, Makeeda returned, then left again for a three-day engagement at a cabaret in Boston, where she was developing a new group of fans.

Laura called the Redevelopment Agency and asked for Bonnie Holland. "Why you calling me at work, Laura? They might get mad at me for this. Ain't supposed to get personal calls. My boss is frowning at me right now."

"Sorry," Laura quickly apologized. "I thought . . . maybe . . ."

"I know what you thought," Bonnie said softly into the phone, her voice peremptory and clipped at first, but then gentle and intimate, a kind of intimacy Laura was familiar with, intimacy they shared from having done the most intimate things together one could do. "I want to see you, too."

"You do?"

"Yes. Can you give me a ride home tonight?"

"Yes!" Laura calmed herself. "I'll pick you up at five fifteen. In front of the building."

"I'll be waiting on the steps, like before. See you then."

Driving Bonnie home, across the Bridge, Laura tried to pretend that there was no awkwardness between them due to the little rejection she had suffered two weeks earlier, when Bonnie clearly had a prearranged assignation going with Butch Blondie, the one Laura had seen her walking and joking with. The worst side of her nature would want to know: d*id she fuck you, did she fist you—I know what a hot little tart you are, and how you probably goaded her into it, or invited her, you little slut—did she fuck you with her strap-on, did she trib you, did she kiss you and tell you how beautiful you are, how she loves your high cheekbones, how sleek your lovely skin is?* All this ran feverishly through Laura's head, but she said none of it. *I have manners*, she thought. I have maturity. *All that stuff is none of my business. I do not own her. I am calm and reasonable. I am no longer the petty jealous type. I have self-control.*

But Bonnie would not let it rest. She wasn't mean about it, but she did want to make Laura a little jealous.

"Don't you want to know about Meredith?" she asked while they were sitting in traffic.

Laura looked out the driver's side window at the little bit of sky she could glimpse over the dark bridge railings. She acted very nonchalant, oblivious. Is that the bitch's name? "Oh . . . who is that? Somebody you work with?" she asked, making a big play out of not caring.

Bonnie smiled slyly. She was not by nature a schemer or a game-player, and so it was a sly but also ambiguously submissive smile. "She's that girl you saw me with. You know, at the BART station." Laura still acted oblivious, and feigned puzzlement. "The one I had over to dinner that night. When you wouldn't stay."

Laura gave her a sharp stare. "I certainly wouldn't have wanted to intrude. To spoil your dinner together."

Bonnie said nothing. She acted like she knew secrets she would not dare divulge, especially now that she knew Laura was a little hostile. They rode in silence for another few minutes. Laura wanted to stop the car and tear Bonnie's clothes off and fuck her passionately on the spot, right there on the Bay Bridge in the middle of snarled traffic. She didn't know why she had this impulse. The more silent and smug and secretive Bonnie became, the more it fanned Laura's lust.

Finally, they cleared the bridge traffic and were only minutes away from Bonnie's apartment. "Okay . . ." Laura said wearily, "I guess you want to tell me about her. So?"

"You were the one who told me to get other friends, Laura," Bonnie said sternly.

"I . . . know," Laura swallowed.

"She ain't as good as you, if that's what you're worried about. But she likes me."

"That's good."

"She likes my black skin, like you do. You white people are strange, but who am I to complain? I like being liked."

Laura could not help smiling over at her. "So do I. I guess that's normal."

She reached over and patted Bonnie's knee. Since LaVonda had got her this new job with the city as a favor to Laura, Bonnie wore skirts instead of jeans, and her shiny black knees were visible, as well as an inch or two of thigh flesh. Laura found her impossibly fetching in her skirts and white tennies. *I'd like to throw 'Meredith' under a BART train,* she thought, *but I'll suck it up and get control of myself if only I can bury my head between these delicious black thighs in about twenty minutes and do the Swiss yodel into your little black sugar doughnut.*

Bonnie again gave her the sly smile, as if she could read Laura's thoughts.

In her apartment, she busied herself clattering pots and pans in her small kitchen, as if dinner were the objective, while Laura stood across the small room from her salivating. And not for dinner. "What are you doing?" she asked Bonnie.

"Don't you want to eat?" Bonnie said, over her shoulder.

"I'm hungry, all right."

Bonnie turned and grinned. "You bad, Laura Robbins. You're a corrupting influence. Heard that on TV. A corrupting influence. You are like a man. You just want pussy. Pussy pussy pussy."

Instead of answering, Laura crossed the small room to the kitchen and took Bonnie in her arms, kissing her smooth cheek. "I want your pussy," she murmured. "Is that so bad? I thought you liked me wanting you."

Bonnie smiled and warmed up quickly, brushing her sensual lips against Laura's cheek too. "I do. In fact, I want to get in bed with you more than anything. It's been too long. You got that wife of yours. I have to make do."

Laura gently pinched her fantastic bottom, though the round moons were so hard it was difficult to get a purchase with her fingers. "It seems like you've been doing all right in that area," she said, sarcastically. What about Butch Blondie? Excuse me, 'Meredith'. "What about Meredith?" she whispered nastily into Bonnie's delectable black ear, before slithering her tongue into it.

Bonnie grinned slyly again. "Meredith likes to fuck me. Does that make you jealous?" She had clearly said it as boldly and unvarnished as possible, hoping to watch Laura's chagrin.

"You know it does."

Bonnie tilted her head flirtatiously. "Good." She smirked. She left the pots and pans where they were and walked into the center of the small adjoining room, toward the wall where the Murphy bed was concealed behind a panel. "Maybe you can show me how jealous you are."

"What's that supposed to mean?" Laura followed her, smiling. She caught up with Bonnie and embraced her again, enjoying the game, forgetting about Meredith completely. Again she ran her hands down to Bonnie's splendid ass and tried to pinch the hard moons.

"If you don't quit doing that, I'm gonna call nine one one," Bonnie said softly, teasingly.

"Oh? And tell them what?"

"That you are trying to rape me."

Laura nibbled and sucked her delicious black earlobe. "Let me get this straight. You're going to tell the mostly male fire department or police department that two black and white lesbians are having a sex quarrel and you need them to rescue you? Right? Maybe we should go downstairs and do it for them on the sidewalk to spare them having to climb two flights."

Bonnie didn't reply. Her eyes looked fierce and defiant, but also playful, and they smoked with sex. She kissed Laura instead, a searing kiss. Laura scorched her right back.

"You're goddamned right it makes me jealous," she panted into Bonnie's cheek.

"Good," Bonnie said again.

Their next kiss was less feverish, more sensual. Laura's tongue explored Bonnie's open mouth deeply. "I like to fuck you, too," she murmured into Bonnie's teeth.

"Have you got one of those strap-on dicks?" Bonnie panted back.

Laura realized that though they had done a lot together, they had never done that. "Yes. In the car," she said, a little breathless with sexual hunger.

"Go get it."

For some reason Laura was almost paralyzed on the spot, and Bonnie had to say it again.

"Go get it. Laura? Go get it."

Laura slowly released her. She nodded. "I'll go get it."

Their eyes were locked together. Laura knew better than to ask why Bonnie wanted her to go downstairs to her car and get the strap-on dildo. She quickly did as she was asked and returned with it in under three minutes, bounding up the stairs so that she was out of breath.

Bonnie had pulled down the Murphy bed while she was gone and stripped back the bed coverings. Laura noticed that she had also adjusted the bureau with the large, swiveling oval mirror so that it would show anything going on in the bed. Bonnie liked to watch. *You scamp!* Laura thought. *You fetching little tease!*

She stood there panting from her climb, while Bonnie laughed softly. "You in some kind of hurry?"

Laura dropped the little valise on the bed and took a step toward her. "Yes," she panted. She grabbed Bonnie and kissed her neck. "I hope your neighbors aren't home from work yet. I'm going to make you scream."

Bonnie smirked sexily. She unbuttoned the top button of her crisp white blouse, her eyes never leaving Laura's. She had somehow transformed herself into this charming little seductress in the months since Laura had first met her, when she had been a friendly though very self-deprecating and unassuming little undiscovered beauty, working in obscurity in an alley sandwich shop, abandoned by her one-time boyfriend, and pretty much expecting little of life. Now she had two women (at least; Laura was sure there must be more, and god only knew how many men) clamoring for her company, and her body. She was confident enough to tempt them with patently seductive measures like this one. Slowly undressing.

You want this body? You want to touch it? You want to see it come slowly into view? You like my black skin, you crazy white girl? Want to see a little more?

Another button unfastened. Laura was hypnotized, watching. Another button. The dark, sleek skin of Bonnie's upper chest was more and more visible. Laura could see the top edges of her white bra cups.

"You are amazingly sexy," she said softly, under her breath.

Bonnie smirked again, salaciously. "What do you like best, my boobs or my ass?" She pivoted on one foot to show off her ass, which Laura already knew was splendid but the spectacular nature of which was concealed pretty effectively by Bonnie's prim skirt.

"Do I have to choose?"

Bonnie shook her head and undid another button. Now her blouse gaped open enough for Laura to see the black skin of her stomach, under her bra. "I already know what you like. I told you. Pussy pussy pussy. Am I right?"

Laura couldn't take any more. The girl was irresistible. She half-lunged forward and grabbed her, crushing Bonnie's mouth with her own, sliding both hands under the cloth of the half-open blouse, letting her fingertips revel in the smooth warmth of Bonnie's skin. "You don't know how much I want you," she panted.

"Yes I do," Bonnie giggled, kissing Laura back. "You gotta get your clothes off too." She started unbuttoning and unzipping Laura just as frantically as Laura was unbuttoning and unzipping her.

In seconds they were down to their underwear. Bonnie's face slid down to Laura's breasts, kissing the tops of them and the not-very-deep cleavage between them, since Laura's breasts were quite small. But Bonnie loved them anyway.

"Take this off," she said, slipping the straps off Laura's shoulders. "You aren't the only one who likes titties."

"Ooohhh, am I being attacked?" Laura feigned alarm. "Am I being sexually assaulted?"

Bonnie giggled softly again. "You are. By me."

She got her mouth on Laura's naked breasts and did not let up, sucking and slurping them thirstily. Laura's nipples ached between Bonnie's sensual lips. It's the new Bonnie, she thought, but did not say it aloud for fear it would stop her. Instead, she held Bonnie's head in both hands, stroking her hair, while Bonnie sucked her vigorously.

"Honey . . . you're making me so wet," she gasped to her.

Bonnie stopped for a moment and grinned up at her. "Me too. Better put that thing on."

"Not yet," Laura said, trying to skim Bonnie's underpants (you really couldn't call them panties) down her hard, sleek black thighs. "I want to rub against you all over first. And kiss you here . . . and here . . . and . . ." She really did not want to get to the actual fucking too fast.

Her words were stopped by one of Bonnie's naked breasts pushing against her lips. She opened them and sucked Bonnie's bulging black nipple inside.

"Oh!" Bonnie gasped. "Yes! Unmh!"

Bonnie's breasts were only slightly bigger than Laura's but lovely little round and very firm balls with thick black nipples, and Laura loved mouthing them with overflowing ardor. She could feast on them for long minutes, while Bonnie gurgled and cooed and hummed in happy pleasure. "You're gonna make me come before you fuck me, if you keep that up," she murmured, settling down into the mattress as Laura switched back and forth between her breasts, sucking each nipple until it was tight and pointing, shiny wet with her warm spittle.

Their bras were both hanging slackly around their arms and Laura's panties were still on, so they quickly divested themselves of the rest of their underwear and began caressing and kissing and writhing together passionately. Bonnie grinned and looked up at the tilted oval mirror, at their entwined naked bodies. She draped a long black arm across Laura's pale back.

"Look at us," she panted.

Laura looked up too. "God, we're beautiful."

"I know."

"We should take movies and sell them."

Bonnie crinkled her nose in a goofy grin. "I'd buy one."

"Me too."

They continued kissing and stroking for several minutes, without looking. Then they looked again. Laura had her mouth full of Bonnie's breast and had to be coaxed to release it long enough to look up at the mirror.

"I wish I had a movie of you when you come, sometimes," Bonnie confessed against her cheek. "You get me hot when you come."

"Honey, you are hot all the time."

"You know what I mean," Bonnie laughed, tickling her. "And you better put that dick on and do me, before I pop."

This was Laura's invitation not only to fasten the strap-on into place and get down to business but also to ask if 'Meredith' had been the one to introduce Bonnie to this new twist. After all, Bonnie seemed so nonchalant about it. Something must've happened.

I always meant to get around to this, she thought as she tightened the harness, but somehow I was always too eager to devour her and eat her alive. And then, she always wanted to be fist-fucked. Couldn't wait for anything else. She kissed Bonnie's shiny dark forehead. "I want to stick my dick into you," she smiled.

Bonnie grinned back. "I guess you're going to get your chance. How come you never did this to me before?"

"I was just wondering the same thing myself." She bit her tongue before saying: It must've been that odious cunt Meredith who got your strap-on cherry before I did. That's enough of that, Laura! she snapped at herself. Stop being so petty and censorious.

And Bonnie made her petty jealousies irrelevant anyway, rolling onto her back and holding her arms up sweetly to Laura, irresistibly sweet, as she always was, pliant and smiling, spreading her sleek black thighs to offer the red, wet crease of her oozing pussy to Laura. "Come and get it," she purred happily.

Laura climbed over one leg and settled in, guiding the head of the shaft toward the puckering, black-lipped slit of Bonnie's beautiful cunt. Bonnie's dark eyes went briefly glassy, and she groaned softly as it slid into her. Laura recalled that she nearly always did this when Laura's hand finally penetrated her pussy, a moment of exquisite sweet sexual discomfort that quickly, very quickly modulated into churning lust. Bonnie gulped breath, and her eyelids fluttered, but then she was looking up into Laura's eyes with deep love. Laura had pushed the shaft as deeply into her as it would go and now was leaning forward over her, dangling her own breasts against Bonnie's, kissing her cheek, her chin, her forehead, her wildly desirable mouth.

"I . . . love to fuck you," she breathed softly into Bonnie's ear, tonguing it passionately. I hate for anybody else to fuck you. She did not say this part out loud. Anyway, you should feel ashamed, she told herself.

Bonnie was already swirling her hips to make the dildo go in and out. "You're . . . pretty good . . . at it," she panted, running her hands up and down Laura's back.

But Laura had done nothing yet, except hold herself stationary while Bonnie gyrated her hips slowly. "You're doing all the work," she whispered, still kissing her everywhere: her gleaming black shoulders, her chiseled collar bones, the underside of her jaw, the secret moist spot behind her ear, down her neck to her throat.

Bonnie smiled. "Then time for you to do some." They rocked gently together in silence for another few minutes, feeling the wonderful sexual tension slowly build. "I like it this way," Bonnie finally said. "I can kiss you and feel your titties against mine, and you can kiss me too. While we're fucking, I mean. I like to kiss while we're fucking."

"Me too." Laura followed up with a dozen hot kisses all over her face.

"It's like fucking with a guy but better," Bonnie panted, growing more aroused by the second.

"Oh . . . you like that, do you?" Laura teased, jabbing her more roughly now with the dildo, sliding one hand down to hold it so that she could deliver more powerful thrusts.

Bonnie did like it. "Unh . . . unh . . . unh!" she grunted softly as Laura fucked her harder, and a little faster. "Shit . . . you're gonna make me come, girl."

"Can you come this way?"

"Oh yes. Oh yes." Bonnie panted, and whinnied softly, bucking under Laura. "Just keep it up that way. Steady. Steady. Oh yes. Ungghhh!"

"But you can't come yet," Laura panted, still kissing every part of Bonnie she could reach with her lips. "Because I'm enjoying this too much. I love it . . . I love it . . ."

Bonnie grinned. "Shut up, Laura, and get to work. You get yours afterward. Unh! Oh! Yes yes! Ungghhh!"

"Not yet!" Laura giggled, even though she was still thrusting seriously. She kissed Bonnie's neck. "Not yet . . . I'm not through kissing you."

But Bonnie was now half-delirious with her crescendo of sex need, pumping and twisting faster and harder, careening toward the finish line. "Ungghh! Ohnnngg! Yes!"

Laura tried to slow it down but that was impossible. She did manage a glance sideways at the mirror, and the sight was so arousing that she could barely tear her eyes away from it. Bonnie's long black arms were wrapped around her paler, creamy body, her black knees and sleek, gleaming thighs were yawning apart with Laura crouched between them, and their groins were churning together in a magnificent, regular rhythm, while Bonnie's pretty face was contorted in a grimace of acute sexual anguish as she hurtled toward her happy explosion. They were entangled and striving and panting and gurgling with joyful, vigorous lust, and Laura wondered if she had ever seen anything so exciting.

She felt a tremor deep in Bonnie's writhing body. "Unnnmmnnn!" Bonnie grunted softly. "Oh!"

"Yes!" Laura gasped into her ear. "Yes, honey, yes!"

Suddenly, Bonnie arched her back and made a little jump up from the mattress, twitching and flexing in a quick spasm. This was following by a fierce howl.

"Auunnnggghhhh!"

She twisted, she leapt up again, she jerked violently in midair, then fell back again to the mattress, emitting a low, guttural moan.

"Ohhnngggmmm! Oh . . . oh shit! Auunngghhhhh!"

Laura had never seen her have an orgasm quite like this one. Or, maybe she had. Bonnie did go in for the violent wrenching and twisting, Laura knew, but in the past Laura had always marked that up to the fisting Bonnie loved so much, assuming that it had brought on these violent spasms. Now she realized this was just the way Bonnie climaxed when super-excited, and she held the quivering girl, not thrusting any more, while the series of spasms worked through her body and began to wane.

"Oooohhhh . . . you had a good one," she cooed into Bonnie's ear, stroking her body tenderly, brushing the hair back from her forehead and kissing away the shiny film of sweat.

Bonnie drifted back slowly from the land of ecstasy, twitching and quivering a little, her limbs still flexing and fluttering, her breath still labored. Laura held her and kissed her. This all went on for long minutes, and they were glued together throughout, the strap-on dildo still deeply embedded in Bonnie's pussy. Bonnie did not respond to Laura's kisses, being too crushed by her orgasm to bother, and then she suddenly did respond, kissing Laura back, coming to life again, stirring, and smiling.

"Nobody like my Laura," she croaked softly, looking deeply, lovingly, into Laura's eyes.

Laura took this to mean that 'Meredith,' no matter how good she might be, was not in the same league with Bonnie's own Laura. This might be a niggling, petty victory, but Laura would take it. Inwardly she smiled, trying not to be smug about it, and wreathed this phrase in her mind with garlands of affection. My Laura. Nobody like my Laura.

They kissed again, deeply, and then Laura carefully extracted the orgasm-maker from Bonnie's clinging orifice, and quickly slipped out of the straps. "Don't you want me to do you?" Bonnie asked softly.

"Yes," Laura said. "I . . . want you to give me the fist." She ran her fingertips along the back of one of Bonnie's shapely black hands.

Bonnie's eyes widened, and a hint of a smile tugged at the corners of her desirable mouth. Incredibly, Laura realized, though Bonnie was wildly partial to the fist, she had never actually returned the favor for Laura, during their relationship. Somehow, like the strap-on, they had simply never got around to it. Mostly, Laura thought, because by this stage I'm so ready to pop that nearly any touch of hers makes me burst.

In fact, this time was no different. She felt so aroused from fucking the delicious girl that even Bonnie's warm breath on her clit would be enough to make her come. But she did want it. She wanted something intense, intimate, and slightly violent, something to match this 'my Laura' moment; a 'my Bonnie' moment. My Bonnie shoved her arm up into my body and made me die of coming. She tried to let all this meaning flood into her eyes as she gazed deeply into Bonnie's.

"What do you think?" she almost whispered.

Bonnie grinned and gently pulled Laura down onto her back. "You sure?" She held up the hand that Laura had been caressing. "My hands are a little bigger than yours."

Laura pulled her down and kissed her, mashing her naked breasts into Bonnie's hard little balls. "Honey, if a baby can get down that chute, I think your hand can make it."

Bonnie giggled softly. "Guess you're right." She frowned, thinking. "You ever have a baby?"

Laura shook her head. "I haven't even been in danger of that for years."

"I almost did once. Had to have . . . you know."

Laura nodded sympathetically.

"He was a total screw-up. A real dick head. I did the right thing."

"I'm sure you did." Laura smiled, fondling Bonnie's world-class bottom with her fingers and watching their bodies in the tilted mirror.

Bonnie saw her looking and grinned. "You like to watch, too."

"I think I could just lie here and have a little orgasm while looking at my pale fingers running all over your dark round ass, my darling. Your skin is so smooth and black."

Bonnie gripped her more tightly, nuzzling Laura's neck. "I think I can make you have more than just a little one," she breathed. "I think I can make you have a big one."

Laura smiled and kissed her nose. "I dare you to try."

Bonnie loved this. Immediately, she began kissing Laura's body, especially her breasts, which she mouth-mauled Laura-fashion for quite a while, showing Laura what she had learned. By the time Bonnie moved further south, Laura was moaning and twisting happily in anticipation of certain further bliss.

"Oh . . . Bonnie . . ." she sighed. "Oh honey . . ."

"Trouble with you," Bonnie murmured, as she began to rub Laura's open, wet pussy with two fingers, "is . . . you get so hot fucking me that you come real fast yourself. Right?"

"Right," Laura gasped, affirming Bonnie's recognition of what she had long known herself. "Oh god . . . yes! Right there! Unhhhh!"

"Now don't you be getting there too fast, Laura," Bonnie warned, in her cutest schoolmarmish tone.

She was kissing Laura's stomach and her inner thighs while she worked a quick three fingers into the juicy warm furrow of Laura's aching pussy. Oh god, this is going to happen so fast! Laura realized.

But Bonnie clearly did not want it to happen fast. It turned out that she wanted to tease and toy with Laura's aroused pussy while watching everything in the mirror, almost as if this were a show they were putting on for her benefit. Laura liked watching it too, but since she was on the receiving end, her responses were mixed. She wanted to watch but was overcome by sharp and ever-growing lust. Bonnie's tongue on her clit made her want to scream with sharp, pent-up fuck-need. She churned and swirled her hips, feeling Bonnie's three fingers slide in and out of her well-lubricated pussy.

"If you . . . don't . . . let me come . . . I'm never . . . going to . . . talk to you . . . again . . ." she panted feverishly, feeling her whole body come alive.

"Oh, you are going to come," Bonnie grinned, now bending more eagerly to the task. "Looks like you are going to come real fast."

"Yes! Unhhh! Yes! Oh!"

Bonnie finally realized that stretching it out further was nearly impossible. Laura was in a frenzy. She writhed and gurgled and begged with her eyes. Bonnie got all four fingers into Laura's pussy, then her thumb too, pushing, pushing, until her hand widened the slippery cavity enough to slip inside.

"Ungghh!" Laura grunted softly, feeling engorged by Bonnie's hand. "Oh . . . shit!"

Bonnie grinned just at the corner of her mouth. "Told you my hand was bigger."

Laura nodded, feeling water spring to her eyes. Often with fist-fucking there was a spellbinding moment of intimacy that enraptured both participants, especially when the full penetration occurred. Bonnie's eyes caught hers, and she knew they were both feeling it, this solemn, stirring moment, and yet as soon as Bonnie began to move her hand it transmuted itself into a crackling, fiery jolt of fierce need that swept everything else aside.

Oh god, fuck me, Bonnie, I'm going to come so hard! Laura thought, beginning to churn her pelvis even more frantically than before. Bonnie, usually on the receiving end of this, knew what was happening and immediately joined in.

"You gonna come, Laura . . . you gonna come now!" she panted, twisting her hand inside Laura's cunt, and thrusting it, thrusting, thrusting, watching Laura's face.

And yet . . . and yet, Laura did not come, not instantly. She felt it building, swelling, throbbing in her body, but not yet ready to burst. Bonnie, completely in tune with her, felt the slight delay too and leaned forward to fervently lick and suck Laura's nipples, grabbing one breast with her free hand and sucking Laura's nipple deeply into her warm, wet mouth.

"Unhhh! Oh!" Laura gasped.

Oh shit! Bonnie siphoning up her nipple like this was just what it took to tip her over the edge. Her whole body clenched in a white-hot, wrenching spasm. She did not even hear the roar that came out of her mouth until it was filling the small apartment.

"AUUNNGGGHHHH! AUUNNGGGHHHH! Oh! Oh!"

"Yessss . . . Laura . . . yesssss!" Bonnie hissed to her, still pumping her hard and rhythmically with her hand, but also catching glimpses sideways of their churning bodies in the mirror.

Accompanying her roar, Laura's pelvis jerked spastically up off the mattress, shuddering in midair, impaled on Bonnie's hand and forearm, spasming wildly in fierce shocks of killing pleasure. The climax knocked the breath out of her. Wheezing and gurgling, she fell back to the sheet, panting and whinnying almost hysterically.

"Mmmmmnnneeeee . . . mnnneeee . . ." she gasped, feeling the wrenching shocks die away almost as quickly as they had arrived. Now she was simply limp, fluttering with helpless feathery little twitches, as the orgasm finally released her. "Oh . . shit!" she finally croaked, her eyelids blinking open to see their merged bodies in the tilted mirror.

Bonnie was also looking and cracked a big grin. "Mmmmm, that worked out pretty well," she said softly. "Too quick . . . but pretty good."

"God . . . the understatement of the year," Laura gasped, still groggy, glassy-eyed.

"Want me to take it out?"

"Leave it in . . . for just a minute, okay? God, it feels so good to have you inside me."

Bonnie was tenderly kissing Laura's body, her stomach, her thighs. "Kind of feels good, doesn't it. I like it when you're inside me."

Laura noticed—though absently, as if in a far corner of her brain—that Meredith had 'left the building.' She was no longer a presence. This act had melded Laura and Bonnie together in an unbreakable union. No one else had a part in it.

Finally Bonnie's lips reached Laura's, and with her hand still embedded in Laura's throbbing pussy, they kissed warmly. "Now . . . you can take it out," Laura whispered at the end of the kiss.

Bonnie did, carefully, and quickly hopped up to get a towel. Then she returned to the bed and cuddled with Laura, both of them again unable to take their eyes off the reflection of their coiled bodies in the mirror.

"We look good," Bonnie murmured against Laura's shoulder.

"We sure do," Laura smiled.

"I wish I wasn't so black, though."

"Why is that?"

"I don't know," Bonnie said, almost wistfully. "Light-skinned sistas get it all."

Laura nuzzled her neck and sucked it, though not hard enough to leave a hickey. "They don't get me. You get me."

Bonnie beamed. Laura could see the fetching little six-year-old she had once been in this beaming, innocent smile. She laid her head on Laura's shoulder. "That's right, I do. Nobody can have you right now but me." She was silent for a few minutes, and they simply basked in the warmth and intimacy of the moment. Then, "You hungry?"

"Why do you ask?"

"Cause I hear your stomach rumbling."

"I guess I could eat, if you feel like cooking."

"Invited you, didn't I? Anyway, you got to fuel up for round two." She rolled sideways off the bed and pulled Laura up too with one hand. "C'mon, you can help. Can you chop onions?"

"I can," Laura said, unable to take her eyes off Bonnie's bewitching naked black body. "You better put something on, though, or I'll be dragging you back here."

Bonnie flirted. "You better," she grinned. She flung a robe at Laura from the closet behind the Murphy bed, and slipped into a loose pale blue cotton nightie of her own that was almost sexier than going naked. "C'mon. Eat first . . . then a little gentle loving, for a change. You wearing me out with that dick."

To be continued...

Miranda Mars

Bonnie Chronicles 4

CONSUMED *by* JEALOUSY

Erotic Lesbian Romance

"I don't think we can see each other anymore," Bonnie said. Out of the blue. Without segué, or even a softening glance. They were sitting in Laura's car outside Bonnie's apartment house in Oakland. Bonnie stared straight ahead, out the windshield.

You let me give you a ride home so you could tell me we can't see each other anymore? Laura wanted to ask her testily, as she tried to recover from her initial shock. She swallowed and tried to keep her pulse from accelerating further.

"Why?" Then, before Bonnie could answer: "Don't tell me. Meredith doesn't like you seeing me."

Bonnie looked straight ahead. Laura wanted to devour her. She couldn't remember a moment in her life exactly like this, but she knew it was true that if a person rejected you, you thereupon wanted that person more fiercely than ever. She had first known Bonnie as a shy, self-effacing but unaffected and gorgeous little sandwich shop girl with a fantastic ass and high cheekbones that made Laura's pussy turn to soup. As a favor to Laura, LaVonda had got Bonnie a job with the city's Redevelopment Agency, and taken a direct interest in getting her to 'dress for success,' and since then Bonnie in her crisp white blouses and neat tailored skirts and tennis shoes with white ankle socks had become a thrilling beacon of lust to Laura. Sitting here now, staring at her profile and wanting to lick every inch of her smooth black skin, as smooth as a baby's bottom, and velvet to the touch, Laura could only struggle to get a handle on her physical desire.

Meredith was a co-worker of Bonnie's at the RDA whom Laura had christened (only to herself) 'Butch Blondie' after seeing them together one afternoon, walking to the BART station. Evidently, she thought sourly, the woman had some charms that were not visible on the surface. She fucks my darling and makes her happy! she thought with a sudden squirt of hot jealousy.

"You're right, she don't," Bonnie broke through Laura's reveries. "She thinks you're using me."

"Using you!" Laura was outraged.

Bonnie turned her head and smiled at her, as if they both knew Laura was a big fraud. "I didn't say it wasn't . . . fun," she said, after searching for a word.

"I'm not using you!" Laura insisted, a little too vehemently.

Bonnie did not stop smiling, though it wasn't a mean or superior smile. "I didn't say I didn't like it," she repeated. "But . . . it makes things kind of difficult. With her."

"Just tell her to get over it," Laura snapped. Honestly! This cunt! Telling my honey who she can see and who she can't.

Bonnie didn't flinch. "She loves me."

"She *loves* you," Laura chortled dismissively. "Right."

"She does."

"So that gives her the right to say you can't see me?"

Laura realized there was a cloudy film of incipient tears in her eyes. Was this her usual stab at cheap manipulation, which she knew she was capable of at such moments? Or was it a genuine upwelling of real emotion, real loss?

Bonnie put a hand on her arm. "Look, Laura. You got your wife Makeeda. Right? And you got LaVonda. You don't see me that much anymore anyway. Right? I . . . got myself a honey, just like you do. You even told me not to wait around just in case you get free. I can't just sit up there waiting for you to have time for me. You see?"

Laura nodded, sniffling.

"It don't mean I'm not grateful for everything you did for me. Getting me this job and all."

Oh? And how about fucking you to ninth heaven about a hundred times! Laura wanted to flash back at her. Control yourself, Laura, you petty jealous little shit, she thought. You are despicable. "LaVonda got you the job," she said, wearily, feeling a dull ache inside her chest.

"She did it because you asked her. We both know that." Dead silence. "Anyway . . . maybe I better go."

Bonnie started to open the door of the car to exit.

"No. Wait." Laura touched her arm. Just the feel of Bonnie's smooth skin against her fingertips was enough to elevate her lust meter into the stratosphere at a moment like this. I'm losing her! I'll never have her again! I want her so badly! I want to hold her, and kiss her!

Bonnie turned her head back, waiting.

"One . . . last kiss," Laura said, in a desperate stab at something, anything to keep her there. It was all so final.

Bonnie shook her head. "Can't do it." She smiled. "You know I can't do it."

"Why? Because then you'll want me?"

Bonnie nodded. "Ain't easy, you know. Saying this to you."

Laura slowly nodded back. "I know." She patted her arm. "Go. Have a good life. I . . . I'll really miss you."

Now Bonnie's eyes welled up with brief tears, even though Laura's had vanished without spilling moments earlier. "Me too."

Then she scooted out of the car and shut the door behind her, walking away toward the entrance to her building without looking back.

Laura's staff assistant came to the door of her small office. "There's someone in the lobby downstairs asking to see you."

"Name?"

"Holland. Ms. Holland."

Laura gulped and tried not to blush. Of course her staff assistant had not the faintest idea who Bonnie Holland was. But Laura nearly fell off her chair. "I'll . . . take care of it," she said, getting up. "I guess I'll just go down there and see what she wants." She smiled tightly at her assistant. "Old friend."

In the lobby, Bonnie was sitting demurely on one of the leather sofas near the security station where visitors were told to wait. Laura had another opportunity to feel little heart pangs and pussy twinges just looking at her from afar in her crisp white shirt and white ankle socks and tennis shoes. And of course her short skirt had ridden up a little, exposing her lovely, glossy black thighs. I've had my head between those delicious thighs, Laura thought as she crossed the lobby and sat down next to her.

"What a sweet surprise," she said, smiling at Bonnie. "To what do I owe this visit?"

She recalled that in the past Bonnie had always been too shy and skittish to actually enter the building where Laura worked, preferring to lurk around the front doors in hopes of catching Laura on her way out. Those had been the days when she had considered herself only a marginal little sandwich shop girl, unworthy of the attentions of someone who dressed like Laura and worked on the twenty-fourth floor for some giant corporation. Now that she was a city employee with a better paycheck and wardrobe herself (thanks initially to LaVonda), she had apparently conquered her fears enough to march right up to the security desk and request an audience with Laura. Well, we've come that far, at least, Laura reflected, thinking again with moderate hostility of Meredith, her enemy and rival for Bonnie's sexual favors.

"I came down here on my lunch hour. Shopping," Bonnie lied, averting her eyes. Laura realized it was noonish. She had temporarily forgotten about her own lunch. "Just thought I'd . . . say hello."

"Well, hello. Hello hello hello," Laura beamed at her. "Maybe if you can wait five minutes, I can go grab my stuff and come back down and join you for lunch."

Bonnie shook her head. "Got to get back. They hate it if you late getting back from lunch. Just . . . wanted to see you, that's all."

Laura's heart melted. It absolutely melted on the spot. So much for that witch Meredith, she thought spitefully. "Maybe . . ." she found herself suggesting, "we could . . ."

What was she going to say? She couldn't offer Bonnie a ride home since she had taken BART to work herself that morning. She paused and dithered in her mind, trying to come up with something.

"You could give me a ride home," Bonnie blurted out, to help her.

"I can't." Laura's shoulders fell. "I'm riding BART too."

"We could ride together," Bonnie offered, smiling.

"We take different trains."

"You could take the Fremont train and transfer at MacArthur," Bonnie, the experienced BART rider, said. "Then we could talk."

"Oh yeah, while we're jammed together like sardines by grouchy commuters."

Bonnie tilted her head and smiled. "Guess you're right."

"I could drive over to your place as soon as I get home," Laura said, hoping she was not being too forward. After all, Bonnie's warmth and furtive show of affection was not grounds for assuming she was suddenly inviting Laura back into her bed. Or was it?

"Better not." Bonnie frowned out of discomfort.

"Meredith?"

She nodded. Then she squirmed on the leather sofa and made as if to get up. "I'll call you. Maybe we can . . . oh, I don't know." Bonnie was clearly at what used to be called sixes and sevens; not knowing where to turn, or what to suggest. In fact, Laura realized, they both were.

As she looked intently at Bonnie, it was hard to misinterpret her meaning. If we were alone and in private, we would be fucking at this very instant, Laura realized. She reached out and took both of Bonnie's slim, shapely, black hands in hers. "You call me," she said, as warmly as possible. "You call me when you feel like it, okay? You call me. I'll be waiting."

Bonnie's eyes glistened. "I shouldn't be doing this," she said softly.

"Yes, you should," Laura said, a little too quickly. "I am so glad you came by. Bonnie, look at me." Bonnie looked up, eyes still glistening. "I will always be your friend. You call me any time, okay?"

Bonnie nodded. After a brief moment of letting her hands linger in Laura's, she stood and walked toward the glass doors of the exit. Laura could not help gazing at her lovely bare black legs and wanting to kiss them. She suppressed a sigh and stood herself, walking slowly toward the elevators.

Bonnie did not call for days. Finally, the phone. "You could come over tonight. After work." A hushed, near-whisper.

Her voice was so soft and distant that Laura could barely hear her. She had plans to go swimming after work, but they were easily broken. "I can be there at six."

"Good," Bonnie said. "Hanging up now. See you then."

This all felt wondrously secretive and sexy to Laura. It was very like the way she felt when she and Sara did it behind Sara's friend Darlene's back, Darlene apparently being fiercely jealous. Apparently Meredith was too. It made Laura feel like these two, Sara and Bonnie, were endangering their current relationships because having sex with Laura was an irresistible urge, something they could not deny themselves.

Considering all the Dubai acquisition rumors at work, and the job uncertainty vapors and innuendoes that swirled around them, depressing in the extreme, it was enough to buoy her spirits temporarily at least, and make her feel desperately wanted. At home before getting in her car and charging over to Bonnie's in Oakland, she did a quick sponge bath and sprinkled a little of the *Ysatis* perfume Shelley had given her long ago on discreet parts of her body. Mustn't smell for my sweetie, she chirped inwardly, having a hard time not singing with joy at this invitation.

Bonnie wants me! She wants me to ravish her and put that witch Meredith in the shade! Oh, I am so going to take her to fuck heaven about nine times!

But when she got there, she found that Bonnie was as nervous and guilty-seeming as she had been the last time, the time she had told Laura they shouldn't see each other anymore. She was stiff and withdrawn, from the moment she opened the door and let Laura into her apartment.

"Maybe this is a mistake," she said to Laura.

Laura saw that the Murphy bed was still undeployed, still concealed behind its panel in the wall. And the old dresser with the tiltable oval mirror that Bonnie always had strategically placed so that you could look up and see the reflection of you and her fucking was pushed back against the wall, in its proper place.

"This is not a mistake," Laura said firmly. "Come here and let me kiss you. It's been ages."

But Bonnie did not move. She was having second thoughts, it was clear. She looked scared.

"What are you scared of?" Laura asked, approaching her.

"I never really cheated on anybody before. I mean, I had guys who cheated on me. At least I'm almost sure they did. But not me. I ain't good at lying. If she asked me . . . I'd have to tell her."

Laura was close enough now to take Bonnie in her arms, which Bonnie allowed her to do without a struggle. Laura brushed her lips against the girl's ineffably smooth black cheek. "God, it's been so long since I could feel you like this," she breathed softly against Bonnie's ear.

"Feels good," Bonnie almost whispered, running her hands up Laura's back.

Laura kissed her mouth gently, slowly, not demandingly. The kiss grew more heated as it went on. Soon Laura was sucking her lips and stabbing her tongue deep into Bonnie's open mouth.

"Laura . . ." Bonnie confessed, even while still kissing hungrily, "I can't help it, I want you to fuck me."

"You don't want it any more than I do," Laura panted into her neck, kissing the smooth black column of flesh up and down. "Here . . . take this off."

She began unbuttoning Bonnie's white shirt.

"Let's get the bed down first."

Together, as they had done so many times in the past, they opened the door panel and lowered the bed. Bonnie pulled down the bed coverings, exposing the sheet. Laura pulled her close again and resumed unbuttoning her shirt. "I want to eat you alive," she panted.

Bonnie giggled. "Hold on there, girl. I ain't going anywhere."

"I want you. You're so lovely."

"I want you, too," Bonnie grinned.

Laura got Bonnie's shirt off and reached behind her to unclasp her bra. Bonnie tried to unfasten the buttons of Laura's blouse, which ran down her back, but Laura was moving too fast for her.

"Hold still," she told Laura. "We both gotta be naked, you know."

"Sorry," Laura grinned. "Here, let me help."

In another minute they were naked, falling onto the bed, coiled together, Laura squeezing and sucking Bonnie's pretty little dark breasts as if they would escape her if she didn't get them both into her mouth as quickly as possible.

"I love your big black nipples," she panted, slurping them thirstily, sucking them deep.

"Unh . . . unh . . . oh shit, Laura, you suck so hard!"

"I can't help it."

Again, Bonnie giggled softly. "That's what I love about you. You really mean it, you can't help it."

"I know." Laura stopped for a moment. "Sometimes I'm afraid I want you too much, and you're going to get tired of it, and . . . turn to someone like Meredith instead." Like when you said *We can't see each other anymore*, she wanted to add.

Bonnie crinkled her nose. "She want me too, you know. You two white girls just can't get enough of this little black girl pussy."

"I'm sorry. I didn't mean to bring her up."

Bonnie frowned, but playfully. She pushed Laura's face back down to her breasts. "It's okay. Just keep sucking and shut up. You make me want to come when you suck me that hard."

Laura resumed happily sucking and squeezing them, but this time not so hard, no matter what Bonnie said. Still, she was never happier than when she had a pretty darling's nipples in her mouth, oral maniac as she was. She sucked them in a transport of bliss, and Bonnie sighed and squirmed and moaned and gazed at her lovingly, smiling as Laura engorged her mouth with her breasts.

"I think we better get to it," she panted after a while, into Laura's hair. "I'm gonna pop before you even touch my pussy."

Laura kissed her way up Bonnie' smooth chest to her mouth. "You want the usual?"

By this they both knew Laura was asking if Bonnie wanted The Fist, for which sexual practice she had the keenest desire, ever since Laura had done it to her the first time. It was, as Laura knew, catnip to certain girls; they could never get enough. She fondly recalled Mavis, and Mavis's sister Brenda, who were devoted to it. And the way Randi had come to love it; and even Sara, the last woman Laura would have guessed could fall into excruciating spasms of coming with Laura's arm halfway up her sweet pussy. And she could understand why. Over and above the acute sexual thrills that came from it, there was in fist fucking frequently a mysteriously deep and emotionally moving component sometimes that made it so piercing one could never get over the need to feel it again. She knew this was the way Bonnie felt.

Bonnie grinned at her, both bashfully and brazenly, if that were possible in one grin. As if not trusting herself to speak, she simply nodded. Laura embraced her and kissed her under the ear, an especially intimate kiss. She nipped her cute little black earlobe at the end of the kiss. You know that witch Meredith can't give you what I can give you, my darling, she thought, sending Bonnie telepathic waves.

"Mmmm, let me suck and lick that beautiful pussy to get it ready for Mama's hand," she murmured softly, kissing her way down Bonnie's lovely young body to her smooth black tummy, pushing her thighs open.

"Don't take too long," Bonnie panted. "Told you I'm close. You set me on fire, Laura."

"Oh, good," Laura smiled. "I like being the match that lights you on fire."

"Unnhhh!" Bonnie gasped softly as Laura's tongue invaded her lovely wet pussy.

For all the loving fist-fucking Laura had given her--oh god! does that horrible dyke to it to her too? she wondered--Bonnie had a very snug and small pussy, though beautifully shaped, and Laura always exulted in tonguing and sucking it with fervent passion, as she was doing now. And Bonnie was right, she was very wet and swollen. Her little pinkish clit was protruding at the top of her slit, all excited and engorged. Laura treated it tenderly with her tongue, though it was hard to avoid the temptation to suck it hard and watch Bonnie explode in a shooting star of coming without warning.

But a more solemn ritual awaited. They had been there before, many times, and revisiting that deeply intimate moment was, Laura knew, a culmination neither of them could destroy.

"Ohhhhh . . . oh god . . ." Bonnie moaned softly, her eyelids fluttering open to glance down her undulating body at Laura's face between her thighs. "Oh god, Laura, you better do it. Please!"

Does she do this to you? Laura was probing Bonnie's tight, buttery slit with two fingers while delicately swiping her engorged clit with her careful tongue. But she castigated herself, promptly. Stop it, Laura! Stop ruining this sweet moment with your despicable jealousies! They are wrecking the mood. This sweet girl is going to come gloriously in a few moments, and nobody counts right now but the two of us. Just us. Come on, honey, take Mama's hand . . . yes . . . take it . . . slowly . . . slowly . . .

With patient, rhythmic tenderness, Laura inched more and more of her wedged fingers into Bonnie's yielding pussy with each thrust. Bonnie's pussy was tight, but also very slippery and wet, and in only a few more seconds Laura's whole hand slipped into the clasping sleeve, up to her wrist. Bonnie did not even see it since her head was thrown back, her neck arched, her marvelous little breasts pushing upward, her taut midriff straining.

"Unhh! Ohnngg! Ungghhh!"

"Oh yes," Laura soothed her. "Oh yes . . . Bonnie, honey . . . you are going to come so hard."

"Ungghhh! Oh . . . shit!"

"Does it feel good?"

"Ungghhh! Do it . . . to me . . . fast! And hard! Oh shit, Laura, I'm going to come so fast!"

"Yes. Yes."

Laura kept up her steady pace and gentle thrusting rhythm. Even though Bonnie said she wanted it hard and fast, Laura knew that Bonnie's own body would govern the tempo. When she began to churn and twist and flex, it would be time enough to accelerate the pace.

Bonnie pushed herself up on her elbows, looking down at Laura's hand thrusting into her pussy, her dark eyes flaming. "Kiss me . . ." she gasped hoarsely. "I need you to kiss me."

"I love to kiss you," Laura said, altering her position slightly so that she could continue hand-fucking the girl while also looping one arm around Bonnie's neck and pulling her upper body closer.

Their naked breasts actually brushed, and Bonnie's mouth seared Laura's with passion. "Unh . . . unh . . . unh!" she half-grunted and half-panted.

And now the inevitable faster churning began to develop, as Bonnie pushed her impaled cunt down onto Laura's thrusting hand, and stabbed her tongue erratically into Laura's mouth, panting and whimpering more and more desperately. The deep, stirring intimacy that they often felt at this moment gave way to an almost delirious fury of clenching and teeth-clashing and guttural panting as Bonnie grabbed Laura's forearm with her hand, something she often did, and jammed her pubic bone down into Laura's wrist, mashing her excited clit into Laura's arm and bucking wildly as the first waves of a killer orgasm began to wrack her body.

"Annggmmhhieee . . . annnggmhhiieeee!" Bonnie suddenly erupted in wailing cries, her entire body shuddering hard against Laura's.

Laura kept her embrace tight, one arm looped began Bonnie's back and pulling her close, as she felt the clasping shocks of the girl's cunt muscles gripping her hand rhythmically, in synch with Bonnie's hot screams.

"Mmnnnggnnneeee! Oh! Oh shit! Mmnnggiieee!" Bonnie wailed, burying her face in Laura's neck as her body began finally to slow down, to unwind, to relax and release itself from the fierce clenching. "Ohhhhhhhh!" she finally sighed, her face still buried in Laura's neck, her breath rapid and harsh.

They had kissed before while fist-fucking like this, but never throughout the entire act, their mouths hungry, their teeth clanking painfully, their bodies pressed tightly together. Something in the kiss, in the entire moment, spoke to Laura of Bonnie's searing inner need, a throbbing desire she had perhaps ignored or minimized before. It made her understand not only Bonnie's clear attachment to her, but also the place Meredith was now assuming in her life. *She loves me*, she had told Laura. This was gratifying . . . and also painful.

No wonder she loves you, she thought, stroking Bonnie's smooth, naked back while she listened to her breathing slowly return to normal. Who wouldn't love you?

She wiggled her hand, as if to remove it slowly from Bonnie's tight pussy.

"No," Bonnie said, into Laura's neck, clasping her more closely. "Not yet." She clung to Laura. "God. It was the best ever."

It had indeed been very moving, albeit bittersweet. Laura smiled calmly and kissed her, now slowly disentangling their bodies. "I'm glad it was so good. But we're both going to get a cramp if we don't sort of . . . you know, separate and clean up?"

Bonnie grinned and nodded, slowly pulling her body away from Laura's, who extracted her hand and wiped it on the sheet. "Want me to get a towel?" she asked Laura.

Laura shook her head. "I want you to hold me . . . and let me hold you."

They stretched out together and embraced, head to toe. Laura ran her fingertips all over Bonnie's delicious young body. They lay that way, silently, for a long time.

Then, without speaking, Bonnie began to return the favor, making love to Laura with slow, deliberate skill, a skill Laura had taught her. When it was over, several minutes later, Bonnie made a point of getting out of bed to pull the old dresser closer and tilt the oval mirror to show their reflections. Laura watched her lovely black body with growing desire.

"I could look at your naked body forever," she said to Bonnie when Bonnie returned to the bed.

Bonnie smiled bashfully. She nodded up at the tilted mirror. "Now you can look at it while you fuck me."

Laura reached out and cupped one of her lovely young breasts in her hand. "Mmmmm, you have turned into such a hot little slut," she purred. "I remember when you couldn't use that word to me."

Bonnie looked down, even more bashful. "I know."

Laura encircled her in her arms. "Come here and get some more loving."

"Okay," Bonnie said, her dark eyes dancing with fresh fire. "You know I'm gonna have to lie about this. She'll ask me for sure."

Laura put a finger on her nose. "At least you won't turn all red, like I do."

"Don't matter. You can tell. She'll be able to tell."

"No she won't. Before I leave tonight, I'm going to teach you to lie with a straight face. It's like playing poker. You just have to believe what you're saying. Like an actor does in a movie."

"Don't know how to do that either," Bonnie grinned.

"Of course you don't. I'm going to teach you."

Now Bonnie even laughed. "Just like you taught me everything else?"

Laura nodded.

"Good. Teach me now."

To be continued...

A Secret Affair

Bonnie Chronicles 5
Lesbian Romance

Miranda Mars

Several weeks had passed since Bonnie, unable to suppress her desire for Laura, had invited her back into her bed for an evening of heated and vigorous reunion screwing.

Even though Bonnie, at the behest of her new lover Meredith, had given Laura the old heave ho, explaining carefully that her feelings had not changed but that Laura was already married, to Makeeda, and that Meredith was seriously jealous of her, Laura had nevertheless been convinced that Bonnie deep down had the same longing for her that she now was feeling more and more acutely. She had to know if that spark they had reignited several weeks ago was still flickering, and on impulse one evening after work, around five when she knew Bonnie would be getting off from her job at the Redevelopment Agency, she drove by the RA building just on the chance she might catch her alone, walking to the BART station.

She was so excited that she had to press her thighs together hard to stop the happy little tingling in her cunt as she drove by the building. It wasn't that sex alone was driving her but instead the deeper longings in both her mind and her body that encompassed her emotional attachment to this sweet girl, whom she, with LaVonda's help, had rescued from her dead end sandwich shop job--the girl LaVonda had derisively called Laura's little 'fuck bunny,' but who in reality was as guileless and shy and charming a little darling as you would ever find. That lucky witch, lucky butch dykey bitch Meredith, Laura swore under her breath as she cruised slowly by the steps of the Redevelopment Agency. No Bonnie.

Since she rarely drove to work any more, only on days when there were meetings away from the office, she had few opportunities to do this. And so it was maybe ten days before she had the opportunity again. Still no Bonnie. Maybe I should call her? No, I'll just get blown off again. 'Meredith doesn't want me to see you.' She made her inner voice, mimicking Bonnie's, as smarmy as possible. 'Meredith doesn't want you fucking me. She thinks I might find out you're better than her.' 'She can't make me come the way you can. She's jealous.'

There was a part of Laura that became very ashamed of herself when she eavesdropped on these silly fantasies of hers. She had good cause to despise Meredith, though she had never even met her, but it was just childish and petulant to be rehearsing these things in her mind, while she cruised the streets around the Redevelopment Agency, looking for her winsome little fuck bunny of the past.

It was over a month of doing this before she finally ran across Bonnie. During this time Makeeda had returned home for a week-long hiatus. There had been another acquisition scare at work, and Laura and her co-workers reluctantly had to come to terms with the notion that their company was clearly in play, and that things might change dramatically almost without notice. One of the cats, Monk, turned out to have dental problems and needed a cat dentist, of all things; which took time and money and added to her anxieties. Her longing to see Bonnie waxed and waned, given these sometimes pleasant and sometimes gnawing distractions, but it was waxing again when one evening after work, she spotted Bonnie, alone, walking to the Civic Center BART station.

Laura drove up beside her and beeped her horn gently. Bonnie, looking amazingly fetching in her crisp white blouse and tight navy blue skirt and sneakers, office attire that LaVonda had painstakingly bought for her to make her more presentable as a civil service employee (formerly a sandwich shop girl), glanced over at the car and at first frowned, not recognizing Laura in the late afternoon shadows. Even though she was not dressed at all in an alluring way, Laura knew the delicious dark body that lay hidden under those prosaic clothes, and she feared she was leering.

She pressed the button to roll down the passenger side window and leaned across the seat, so Bonnie could see her better. "Oh. It's you," Bonnie said.

This was a bit deflating. "Well, you could be a little more pleased to see me."

Bonnie cracked a slight grin. "Right. I am. What are you doing here?"

"Looking for you. Is Meredith going to pounce? And shred me to bloody pieces like a harpy?"

Bonnie glanced up and down the street at the traffic. "You better pull over somewhere if you don't want to get a ticket."

"Why don't you hop in? I'll give you a ride home."

Bonnie pointed to a bus stop ahead, an indentation in the curb, where Laura could pull over. She walked up and leaned into the open window again. "You'll get a forty dollar one here if you stay for long."

"Get in. Please."

Bonnie nodded, then looked both ways, as if trying to make up her mind.

"She won't see you if you hurry up," Laura prompted.

Bonnie got into the car. "She ain't even here. She's in Montreal. Her mama got cancer or something."

This momentarily deflated Laura once again. Oh shit, here I am hating her, and her mother's got cancer. "I'm sorry to hear that," she said in measured tones, so that Bonnie would realize she was sincere. She pulled out into the traffic. "Does this mean you're accepting my invitation for a ride home?"

Bonnie grinned sheepishly at her. "Guess so. Long as it doesn't mean anything else."

"Whatever else could it mean," Laura said acidly, pulling out into the traffic.

It was about five minutes before Bonnie responded to this. They were halfway across the Bay Bridge by then, sitting in slow traffic on the bottom deck.

"Could mean you want to do what we used to do," she said calmly, looking out the window toward the Port of Oakland, not at Laura.

Laura grinned sideways at her. "Who wouldn't want that? You aren't exactly the ugly duckling, with your cute sneakers and your tight skirt. And your Choctaw cheekbones and your beautiful skin."

Bonnie said nothing. She caught Laura looking down at her legs, but then looked back at the Port of Oakland again.

"You only got one thing on your mind, Laura. I had a boyfriend like you once. Pussy pussy pussy."

"Not true," Laura protested, acting wounded. "I really like you. Miss you. Did I ever tell you about how my heart used to flutter in the old days when you were working in the sandwich shop and you used to let your fingertips linger in my hand when you made change for me. And my heart went flippity flop?"

"Yes. Several times."

Well, that squelches that one, Laura thought. So much for sentimental attachments. She reminded herself that Bonnie had done that to everyone, that sweet gesture with the fingertips, and that it meant nothing special to her; it was just a habit. Laura could read into it whatever she liked, but Bonnie was not going to be seduced by her little private memory, which she had misinterpreted anyway.

By the time they reached Bonnie's small one-room apartment by Lake Merritt, Laura was deep in the throes of desperately wanting her, the more desperately because she knew she was being held at arm's length. It was as if the long arm of The Possessive Dyke, Meredith, was reaching out to grasp Bonnie all the way from Montreal precisely to keep her from Laura's lecherous clutches. As if to emphasize this feeling, Bonnie said,

"You can't come up. Sorry."

"You are not sorry. You might as well be honest." Laura pouted. She was not above a cheap manipulation, she knew.

Bonnie looked at her squarely, and even smiled. "No, I really am. If things were different . . . you could come up. But I would feel like I was cheating."

Sometimes cheating can be fun, Laura wanted to tell her. "What if I have to pee?"

Bonnie frowned at her with scorn and disbelief. "I'd think you were lying. You tried that before once. Remember?"

"Cross my heart," Laura said, doing it with her forefinger, smiling brightly. How can you turn down this face? I made you pant.

Bonnie shrugged. "No hanky panky. You pee, you go. Okay?"

"Bonnie, you're so mean. Cross my heart," Laura said again.

In Bonnie's cramped little studio apartment, she immediately noticed that the old salvage shop dresser with the swiveling oval mirror, which during her own time with Bonnie had always been pulled over catty corner to the bed so that they could watch themselves fucking, was back against the wall. Mmmm. Is that because you don't especially like looking at her ugly, lumpy, squarish, overweight body while she's doing you? she thought spitefully of asking.

She used the toilet quickly, then found Bonnie across the room in her small kitchen, which was blocked off from the rest of the room by a three-foot-long countertop. "Remember when you used to make slumgullion? After we--"

"Don't say it, Laura," Bonnie interrupted her. "I know what we did." Bonnie's pretty face was stony and unmoved.

"I loved it. That's all I wanted to say. I . . . loved all of it."

When Bonnie looked up from whatever she was doing--making a salad--her black eyes were, surprisingly, wet and shiny. Laura smiled at her.

"Me too," Bonnie said softly, looking down again, tearing lettuce leaves into a glass bowl.

"Can I help?"

"You hungry?"

For your sweet pussy, I am, Laura wanted to say. But she knew Bonnie already knew that. "I could eat a little salad, if that's what you're asking."

She came around the countertop and stood behind Bonnie, then raised her hands and rubbed Bonnie's neck and shoulders with her fingers while Bonnie continued to tear lettuce. Bonnie had always worn short hair, and there was plenty of lovely black neck exposed. Laura wanted to lean forward and kiss her cheek, or tongue-tickle her marvelous black ear, but didn't dare. Bonnie said nothing and pretended not to notice that Laura was giving her a massage, a gentle, loving one.

Soon she finished with the lettuce and looked inquisitively back over her shoulder. "That feels good," she said softly.

"I'm glad," Laura smiled.

"But I've got to cut the tomatoes."

Laura removed her hands from Bonnie's shoulders and stepped back a little. Bonnie turned to face her. "Just one kiss?" Laura asked, trying to appear as innocent as possible. "It's been so long."

Bonnie nodded. "I know. But you're married. I don't want to be kissing you."

"Yes you do."

Bingo. Bonnie was caught. She knew Laura could see it. But she didn't reply. She was caught. She could not deny it. Laura knew she had to grab the moment and leaned forward, letting her lips brush Bonnie's full, sensual mouth. Purest heaven!

At first Bonnie did not respond; but then, she did. Her lips moved under Laura's light brushing. They brushed Laura's back. Laura could feel Bonnie's warm breath on her mouth. Her heart was nearly melting. God, I hope hers is too! she thought.

Bonnie did not close her eyes, and because of that Laura exerted herself to keep hers open too. They were locked in a deep soulful stare. Finally, Bonnie whispered, her lips so close to Laura's that she could not form words without their mouths touching again.

"I want you to fuck me," she whispered.

Laura could not keep her eyes from closing in happiness for the briefest instant. She was not much of a believer, but her prayers had been answered. "You don't want it any more than I do," she breathed.

And now their mouths met in a deeply emotional and searing kiss. A long kiss, a searching, soon ravenous kiss. They were both panting a little when their mouths came apart. Bonnie's fingers were still biting into Laura's back through her blouse. She actually broke into a smile. "Help me move the mirror over to the bed."

Laura gave her a half-grin. "You nasty little thing. You want to watch."

Bonnie reached down and took Laura's hand, drawing her out of the small kitchenette into the main room, over toward the old dresser with the tilting oval mirror. Together they pulled it out from the wall and turned it a little so that they could tilt the mirror in the proper direction. Bonnie even sat briefly on the bed and looked at her reflection in the mirror to make sure it was right. Then she stood and began to unbutton her crisp white shirt.

Laura stopped her, brushing her fingers away from the buttons. "Here . . . let me do that." She grazed Bonnie's phenomenally smooth black cheek again with her lips. "You know how I like to undress you."

Now Bonnie grinned shyly again and would have blushed, Laura knew, had she not been so black. By the time Laura got the third button undone, she could glimpse the bright floral pattern of Bonnie's bra. "Ooohhhh, look at this pretty thing," she said.

This had to be the odious Meredith's influence, since Bonnie had always been a utilitarian dresser, wearing simple outer clothes, and even simpler ones underneath. Laura bent her neck and kissed the shallow cleavage between her lovely little breasts, still concealed by the flowery bra cups. "I want to see you in your pretty underwear," she murmured, quickly undoing the rest of the buttons, then unzipping Bonnie's little navy blue skirt.

Laura's blouse unbuttoned in back, and Bonnie, who had long arms, was unbuttoning it too, while Laura undressed her. "This is like the old days," she said softly, against Laura's cheek, almost diffidently, as if afraid to bring up the 'old days.'

"Better," Laura purred. "Because we know each other so well. We know how to please each other. Look at these wonderful panties. Bonnie . . . you could be a model. Your delicious body in this beautiful underwear! Mmmm, I love your skin," Laura continued to purr softly, running her lips all over Bonnie's delectable near-nakedness, kissing her cleavage again, and her gleaming black shoulder, and her neck and collarbone. "I love to kiss it. And lick it."

Bonnie was beautifully formed, not lean and tapered like Frankie and Gina, but nearly as black as they were, her body thicker and shorter but with pretty round high breasts and below her narrowing waist a truly spectacular bottom, which Laura had kissed and sucked and love-mauled on many occasions, and was keen to do again. Right now.

She tugged down the elastic band of Bonnie's skimpy floral panties, silky and covered with a brightly colored design. "Whoa . . . slow down there a little, Laura!" Bonnie yelped playfully, dancing away from her momentarily, but not far. "Slow down, girl. You can have it. You don't have to take it all at once."

"Oh yes I do," Laura gasped, now reaching behind Bonnie's back, embracing her really, to get her fingers on Bonnie's bra clasp. "You are so lovely. So hot. I love your body."

Bonnie stood a few inches away and grinned at Laura in disbelief. "You haven't even mentioned how you love my cheekbones," she taunted Laura, teasing her, showing Laura a profile, both sides, of her face. "You know, Meredith has never even mentioned them. Even once. I don't even think she notices."

"Of course she does," Laura said, for some reason apologizing for the horrid Meredith, whom she thought was just stupid and dense enough not to notice. "Who could not notice your beautiful Choctaw cheekbones?" She touched Bonnie's pretty face with her fingertips.

Bonnie had a Choctaw ancestor a few generations back who had bequeathed her these fantastic cheekbones, and Laura had rhapsodized about them in the past. She sparkled and beamed as Laura caressed them with her fingers.

"Here, let me kiss each one," Laura drew her closer.

Bonnie patiently let her. "You are the silliest person I ever went to bed with, Laura. But I really miss you."

By this time Laura had got her bra unclasped and was quickly removing it. She filled her hands with Bonnie's marvelous warm naked breasts, so springy and firm and round. "Mmmm, I love these."

"If you don't get naked too, I'm not letting you kiss them," Bonnie warned, now redoubling her efforts to get Laura's clothes off.

The two of them, already only half-clothed by now, were naked in seconds, and running their hands hungrily over each other's body. Laura's hands dropped directly to Bonnie's scrumptious ass and began kneading and pinching the hard round cheeks. Bonnie cupped Laura's small breasts in her own hands, marveling at the pale flesh under her spidery black fingers. She kissed Laura's neck with a little more passion that Laura was ready for.

"Don't give me a hickey, honey," she panted. "It'll show at work."

Bonnie giggled. "Maybe you'll have to wear a scarf."

Laura pinched her bulbous bottom, and Bonnie danced away, giggling more than ever. "Don't you do that! You can't pinch my ass!"

"Why not?"

Bonnie was more coy and playful than Laura had ever seen her. "Because then you'll have to kiss it."

"Oooohhhh," Laura cooed. "Terrible punishment." She advanced on Bonnie, who was only about three steps away. "I'm going to do more than kiss it," she threatened.

But Bonnie grabbed her hand before she could carry through on her threat and drew her over to the bed. She embraced Laura and pulled her down on the sheet. "Want you to fuck me. Let's do it. I'm horny for you."

"Oh Bonnie." Laura was nearly overcome with emotion.

It seemed a matter of the sharpest urgency to get one of Bonnie's lovely little highly placed breasts into her mouth as quickly as possible. This she accomplished at once, sucking one of Bonnie's shiny black nipples in deep, with almost too fierce a passion. She could feel Bonnie writhe and twitch, and a low gurgle of pleasure escape from her throat.

"Unngghh!"

She looked down at her breast in Laura's mouth, lots of flesh as well as her nipple, and her eyes rolled up as Laura sucked her with keen, deliberate hunger.

"Do the other one!" she panted, pulling slightly away, then pushing her other breast against Laura's mouth. "Shit . . . you suck hard! I love it!"

Rarely so aggressive, she rolled Laura onto her back and straddled her, leaning forward and down so that she could push her breasts into Laura's face. Then she threw her head back and rocked in a rhythm of ecstatic bliss as Laura sucked and squeezed and mouth-mauled the firm round beauties.

"Ohhhnnnnn! Ohhnnnn!" Bonnie moaned, loudly, unable to control her wild physical pleasure.

Laura sucked her hard and also got her hand down into Bonnie's wet crotch, sliding two fingers up into the greasy warm channel of her flooding pussy, and rubbing her distended clit with the fleshy upper portion of her palm.

"Unh . . . unh . . . unh!" Bonnie gasped softly, gyrating her hips to push her pussy into Laura's hand harder. "Oh shit . . . you make me so hot, Laura! Unh! Unh! Do me with your hand! I need it!"

Laura knew well what Bonnie needed. She loved being fist-fucked. Laura knew few other women who loved it as much, and she had a feeling that Bonnie's current partner, the horrid Meredith, did not completely fulfill Bonnie's needs in that particular line. Laura, on the other hand, had a small, accommodating hand and an exuberant desire to please; she would never turn down the opportunity, especially since fisting, in her experience, inspired a mysterious intimacy between the participants that yoked them together in a stirring, thrilling moment of physical and emotional rapture. At least that was the way it was with Brenda, with whom she was now doing it on a semi-regular basis, and with Bonnie, with whom she had not, because of Meredith, done it in a while.

"You're just a nasty little pervert, aren't you?" she purred into Bonnie's saliva-wet, swaying breasts, taking a brief moment off from trying to swallow them.

"Yes!" Bonnie hissed, taking this tease more seriously than Laura had intended. "Please!"

"Mmmmm, how could I deny my baby what she wants?"

Now Laura rolled Bonnie easily over onto her back, kissing her with feverish passion, glimpsing their reflection in the tilted mirror as they embraced, and watching Bonnie's eyes flutter open to watch them too. It was truly a vision. Laura wished she had a recording of it to watch over and over again, whenever she was bored, or down in the dumps. She could see their contrasting naked flesh intertwined and coiled and squirming and even writhing, see them kissing, sucking, probing, see their uncontrollable wincing or smiling or grimacing in sharp pleasure. Bonnie looked even blacker than she actually was when viewed against the bright white sheets, or the paler peach of Laura's naked body, and Laura could not get enough of the sight. She paused, transfixed by the vision of her body interlaced and thoroughly entangled with Bonnie's, her hand on Bonnie's breast, her mouth on Bonnie's gleaming black shoulder, her fingers trailing across Bonnie's taut black midriff, down, down, past the fringe of tight black curls above Bonnie's sweet, gaping, hot pink pussy.

"I am so going to fuck you to heaven, honey," she murmured to her, kissing Bonnie's naked body everywhere as she slowly descended between her yawning thighs.

"Mmmmm . . . mmmmm . . ." Bonnie hummed softly in a half-demented, half-sexually crazed way, her fingers fluttering over Laura's back and her hair and her shoulders, her lovely young body undulating gently under Laura's fervent kisses.

Laura already had two fingers inside the slippery warm sleeve of Bonnie's tight little pussy, and she began sensually licking the swollen little berry of her clit as she slipped in two more to join them.

"Oh yes! Oh yes!" Bonnie gasped softly, in a distant, almost ethereal voice, all her sexual arousal concentrated in one or two little gasps of excitement.

As soon as the wedge of her hand slipped finally into Bonnie's tight, greasy slit, so that it was actually inside her up to Laura's wrist, she could feel a barely perceptible change come over them, sweeping them along, it seemed, in a slow, sensual, undulating sexual magnetism that quickly enveloped their bodies, and their emotions. Bonnie felt it too.

"Oh . . . god!" she gulped softly, her lovely smooth dark body beginning to writhe in slow waves as Laura carefully began to fuck her.

She knew they would both be out of control, especially Bonnie, in only seconds, so she took this brief opportunity to kiss her again: her breasts, her nipples, her gleaming shoulders, her collar bones, her taut, flexing midriff. Her hand moved only infinitesimally inside Bonnie's cunt, twisting a little, pumping a little, gently, deliberately. Bonnie never took long to come this way, but Laura wanted to draw it out for both of them as long as she possibly could.

Since Laura was now frequently doing this with Brenda again, Brenda the expert, she had taken over Brenda's approach too, which was to kiss and rub her partner's clit with her free hand while her other one was plunging in and out of her pussy. This made Brenda, and Laura herself, when it was being done to her, come in about half a minute, so intense and wild were the sensations. She did it with Bonnie, and Bonnie began to yelp and buck and twist and writhe in a frenzy of need.

"Unnngghh . . . mmmnnuunngghh!" she grunted and groaned softly, biting her full lower lip, bucking her hips, tweaking her hard, rubbery nipples, still damp with Laura's fresh spittle, in her frenzied fingers. "Oh yes! Oh yes! Kiss me . .. Laura!"

But Laura knew that Bonnie was going to come before she could kiss her. Both of them were by now being engulfed and overwhelmed by not only the physical whirlwind of this heated fucking, but also by the wave of intimate emotion they had felt with each other from the start, long ago, when engaging in this very act. She could see it in Bonnie's eyes, whenever her eyelids fluttered open long enough to glimpse it there: a stirring, incandescent throbbing that met its equal in Laura's own transfixed, throbbing stare.

"Oh honey . . . oh honey!" Laura panted. "Give it to me. Give it to Mama.!"

"Ungghh!" Bonnie, as she often did, reached down to Laura's wrist, the one protruding from her pussy, grabbed it, and pumped Laura's hand into her faster, more violently, more desperately. "Ungghh! Ohhhnngg! Shit! Ungghhh!"

Her eyes rolled up. Her body flexed, shook, convulsed. Hot little peeps came from deep in her chest as a cataclysmic grimace clutched her features. Laura could feel the quaking inside her pussy, the hot clasping against her fingers and knuckles, before the storm struck.

"AAWWWOONNNGGGG!" Bonnie suddenly cried out, in a roar louder than Laura had ever heard from her, even in their most rapturous moments in the past.

Bonnie stretched, rolled halfway onto her side, one forearm crossed over her face, her body still flexing and undulating as wave after wave of orgasmic shock poured through her.

"Ohnngg! Ohhnnngg! Mnnneeeee! Oh shit! Mnnneeee!"

She kept coming, and Laura simply beamed and held her arm steady so that Bonnie could milk every last scintilla of pleasure out of this thrilling moment. And Bonnie did. After a few seconds she stopped pumping herself with Laura's forearm, and her body went slack, but she did not release Laura's arm from her hand, which was still locked around Laura's wrist, just where it protruded from Bonnie's engorged pussy. Her eyes were streaked with red when her eyelids popped open, and she glowered at Laura with fierce love and lust all swirled together, this just before her head plopped back into the sheet and she turned her face to the side to swoon briefly in the aftermath of her stunning climax.

It either was, or it matched, the most searing sexual moment they had ever shared, and it also throbbed with the emotional connection they had together, a bond that Bonnie's lover Meredith (that shit Meredith, as Laura liked to think of her) had tried vigorously to sunder. Here she was with her arm up Bonnie's tight, clenching pussy, throbbing in unison with her as she skimmed the turbulent waves of a shattering orgasm, and thrilling to each moan and each new spasm.

But it could not last forever. Finally, Bonnie blinked, and came around. She gasped softly and winced slightly as Laura eased her wet hand out of her body. "I'll . . . get a towel," she said in a soft, hoarse voice.

"No," Laura said, catching a glimpse of their naked bodies in the oval mirror as she rolled sideways off the bed. "I'll get it. I know where they are."

In the pre-Meredith days, she told herself, we fucked our brains out here in this very room a hundred times. Don't you remember?

When she returned with a couple of towels, Bonnie was still groggy, but stretched out magnificently across the small bed, buck naked and wildly desirable to Laura, who quickly wiped her hand dry and then flung herself in a fiercely passionate embrace on the poor girl, clasping one of Bonnie's hard, sleek, black thighs between her own and pumping her pussy up and down on it with wanton hunger. Bonnie, caught by surprise, enthusiastically grabbed her back and jammed her hard thigh up into each of Laura's wild lunges, until Laura was wailing and whimpering and shuddering through a wrenching orgasm of her own, burying her face in Bonnie's neck and keening with sharp, jolting, blissful shocks.

When it was over, and Laura lay panting beside her, she noticed that both she and Bonnie seemed somehow embarrassed by the sheer heat and power of the sexual acts they had just performed. She turned and smiled at Bonnie, her breath still coming in short burst, but beginning to return to normal. "That was . . . good," she panted. "That was so good."

Bonnie grinned sheepishly. "It was better than good, Laura."

"I know."

Bonnie snuggled closer to her, so that their naked bodies could touch again. "Maybe we can squeeze in one of these now and then," she said softly, kissing Laura's mouth softly too.

"She--" Laura began, meaning to interject some poisonous remark about Meredith, but Bonnie put a forefinger against her lips.

"Don't say anything about her," she said, becoming suddenly more assertive than Laura had ever seen her be. "She is really a nice person deep down, Laura. You have to accept that. She loves me. You want to deprive me of that?"

"No. Of course not."

"She can't fuck me like you do . . . but then, probably nobody can." Bonnie looked both glum and then resigned in the same moment. "You taught me . . . and you ruined me. I need it from you once in awhile. But remember," she reached down and brought Laura's left hand up to her lips. She kissed Laura's knuckles. "You're married. You have someone who comes first." She kissed them again. "Me too."

"I know," Laura said, chastened. She hugged Bonnie, becoming suddenly sexually aroused again by the feel of Bonnie's firm round naked breasts mashing against her own. "As long as you make a space for me now and again."

Bonnie gave her a sexy and invitational grin. "I think I'm making one for you now," she purred into Laura's bare shoulder. "Leastways the river is starting to run."

Laura kissed her and caressed her lovely bottom with her fingertips. "Mmmm, the most beautiful ass in Oakland," she hummed.

Bonnie giggled. "You obviously ain't been walking around this neighborhood much, Laura."

"They can't be any better than this one."

"I bet you're just like a dude. You want to fuck it, don't you."

"Moi?" Laura teased. "Perish the thought."

"I might let you, if you promise to be gentle."

"You're kidding."

Bonnie shook her head. "Meredith, who you hate so much, taught me how to do it. I kind of like it . . . when it's gentle."

"Really?"

"See!" Bonnie laughed. "You *do* want to."

"Only if it'll make you come like last time."

"Guess I have to leave that up to you, don't I," Bonnie said bluntly, following it with a warm, then passionate kiss. "I'll get the stuff out of the drawer."

The End

Here is a sample from another story you may enjoy:

Hot Lesbian Erotica

MIRANDA MARS

LAURA
And
Arthell

Chronicles Compilation

Over a week elapsed before Arthell could keep her promise to have lunch with Laura in the city. By then, it was difficult for Laura herself to arrange it. When she had initially invited Arthell, she had known what free time she had coming up, but the following week was a hell of meetings and events. Finally, they were able to agree on a day, and Arthell arrived at Laura's office shortly after eleven a.m.

About two weeks had passed since Laura's visit with Amber to the campus, and although she had easily remembered that Arthell was lovely and sweet, she apparently had forgotten how lovely. Arthell wasn't conventionally gorgeous but instead so fresh and wholesome and pretty and healthy looking, with a broad, open smile displaying her even, blinding white teeth, that Laura's heart filled with happiness as she saw her waiting by the guard desk in the lobby, where they held visitors.

"God, I'm so glad to see you!" she blurted out, then felt guilty that she had been too exuberant or obvious in her joy.

She glanced over to see if the guards were looking at her oddly, but they had their hands full with other guests. Arthell did not seem taken aback. She beamed at Laura as if she were happy to see her too.

"I'm so nervous," she said, looking around the lobby. "I've never been to a place like this before."

Laura took her arm. Though it was unseasonably warm outside, Arthell was wearing a thick, ivory-colored, cable knit turtleneck sweater which--unfortunately for me, Laura reflected--covered up a lot of her but also looked enchanting against her smooth dark brown skin and made it look even darker. The sweater was not especially tight but it also emphasized Arthell's lovely jutting young breasts. Laura was swimming in mild lust and happiness as she escorted the girl up to her office.

In order not to seem--to herself, at least; and certainly not to send out veiled hints to Arthell or others in the office--that she was only interested in fucking the lovely, fresh, wholesome young girl, Laura bent over backward to acquaint Arthell in detail with the business and Laura's role in it. She took her everywhere and introduced her to many fellow workers, explaining the point of Arthell's visit, even suggesting to her friends in personnel that they might like to take her name for future reference, maybe for an intern position. Arthell was deeply flattered and grateful.

The more open and flattered and attentive she was, the more Laura wanted her. For lunch they went to a trendy restaurant where the most stylish office workers in the city gathered, and the noise level was so high that you could barely understand your table mate's conversation. Laura gazed into Arthell's dark, unsuspecting eyes. Good thing I'm already in love, she told Arthell in her deep mind fantasy, because if I wasn't I'd be in real danger of losing my heart to you, you sweet, gorgeous thing.

Back to work. Laura took her to a meeting. Arthell sat in a chair back along the wall of the conference room and actually took notes.

"I saw you writing," Laura teased her when it was over, nudging her elbow. "What were you writing? How could you find anything to write down? It's so boring. I have to go to those things all the time."

"I saw you writing too," Arthell beamed.

"Only to save my ass," Laura said under her breath. "And to have something to do so I don't look bored."

"I didn't think it was boring at all," Arthell said, totally honest. "I thought it was exciting."

"Wait till you have to sit through three or four of them a day," Laura said.

She looked at her watch. She had been self-disciplined so far, but it was getting harder. She wanted to grab Arthell and kiss her hungrily, every minute she was with her. For a few seconds she lost sight of the fact that Arthell had displayed no inordinate affection for her, or sent any other overtly sexual signals, so that an embrace would probably be sharply repelled. Still, she could hardly bear the urge to do it.

"Look, it's almost three," she said. "I'm not going to get anything else important done today. Why don't I take you to my place, so you can see where I live? Then we can hit the bridge and get you back home, before the true rush hour crunch gets going."

Oh god, please say yes! she thought. I want you so much! But I promise not to make a pass at you if you just give me one little sign that it won't work. Promise. I don't need the ego pain, and I wouldn't have you think ill of me for the world.

"Sounds cool to me," Arthell smiled, flashing Laura with her perfect white teeth.

Arthell's legs were long and thin and dark brown and smooth. Laura had never noticed her legs, unbelievably, until now when she was sitting next to her in the car. During her visit to the college, Arthell had been wearing baggy pants. Now she was wearing a skirt, but Laura had kept her eyes discreetly away from her legs, not wanting to appear too obviously interested in any part, especially an exposed part, of Arthell's delicious young body.

But now, as she drove, she could hardly keep her eyes from darting down to them. They were not really well-shaped, the part from the knee down anyway, but very thin, and yet she wanted desperately to rub her cheek against them. She controlled herself by scrutinizing the traffic, and soon they arrived at her condo.

Safely inside, she threw her coat and purse on a chair and heaved a sigh, really a sigh of relief though she tried to disguise it as being merely a sigh of weariness after a day in the office. "How about a glass of iced tea?"

Arthell smiled. "I could use one. It's a little hot out there today."

"You must be hot in that sweater."

Arthell grinned ruefully. "I thought it was always cold in the city."

Laura nodded. "Usually. This heat is weird. I could get you something to wear if you want to take it off. Something a little lighter."

Oh god! she thought. She could feel her pussy pulsing and itching and creaming a little. Don't get ahead of yourself, Laura.

Arthell shrugged. "I guess we won't be here that long."

"You could just keep it and give it back the next time I see you." Laura tried not too obviously to press her advantage. "Really . . . why not."

"Oh . . . okay. I guess it is a little hot."

"Come with me."

Laura took her into the bedroom. As soon as she did, she thought better of it. Oh damn, if I try to kiss her or anything in here, it will look so planned. It will look like the only thing I want is her pussy. Like I invited her here just for that. So I could make a pass. What a horny old devious shit you are, Laura. Old enough to be her big sister.

They looked through her drawers and found a thin, blue, ribbed cotton sleeveless top for Arthell to wear.

"We're about the same size," Laura said, taking the opportunity to look at Arthell's marvelous young body, as if gauging their similarities. "You have a little more umphhh up here, that's all," she smiled, making a playful little shelf with her fingers under her own small breasts. "I think it'll fit."

"Me too," Arthell nodded. "God, I love your bedroom." She looked around. Laura smiled, having tidied it up purposefully this morning before leaving for work. "You live here all alone? What about your cat? I haven't seen her."

"My cat?"

"You know, Rhonda. The one you said would scratch your eyes out if you didn't get home to feed her. I'm allergic to cats, but I don't seem to be having a reaction. I was a little worried about it when you invited me here." Laura vaguely recalled having told her something about an imaginary cat when they had first met, in her hurry to make excuses and get away after being sorely tempted to make a pass at the sweet young thing.

"Oh . . . the cat," she stammered awkwardly. God, the cat. I forgot completely about telling her that. "I had to give her away. I . . . wasn't home enough to keep her company. She kept getting lonely. And fat. I had to give her away."

"That's sad. I love cats. You must've had professional cleaners. I don't smell any cat dander around anywhere."

"Oh . . . yes . . . I did," Laura stammered again, wanting desperately to change the subject. "Well . . . just put this on. I'll wait for you in the living room. In fact, I'll get us some iced tea."

Laura wanted to hang around and watch her change and was hoping that Arthell would say: Don't bother to leave. I'm not the modest type.

In a way she couldn't help being reminded of her first girl, Karen, and how Laura had unintentionally glimpsed her naked body when Karen was changing into a bathrobe Laura had offered her, after they had both been caught in the rain and Karen's clothes were soaked. It had been the beginning. She had never looked back, and here she was hoping to look at Arthell's naked body, or near-naked body anyway, and feeling more and more like a disgusting voyeur.

This feeling of revulsion and anger at herself propelled her quickly into the kitchen, where she mixed up a pitcher of iced tea in a fit of concentration, willfully expelling from her mind the thought of the darling Arthell half-naked in her bedroom, slipping into one of her own tops. Arthell reappeared moments later, carrying her thick white sweater in one hand. The cotton top Laura had loaned her clung much more to her body and emphasized the thrilling curve of her breasts. Again Laura could see the outline of her bra straps through the thin fabric.

"I'll bet that feels better," Laura said, handing her a tall glass of iced tea. "Just put it over there on the chair where we won't forget it."

They sat and talked. Laura felt very odd. She realized how weird it was when two people had completely different agendas and yet were pretending to be on the same wave length. Arthell had nothing on her mind but absorbing Laura's external lifestyle, probably fantasizing about how one day soon she too would be a single working girl, happy, surrounded by nice things, living in her own neat condo, pulling down some respectable bucks working for an exciting business firm.

Laura, on the other hand, was looking for a moment of opportunity. She didn't want to let this moment pass, as the last one had when she had dropped Arthell at home after first meeting her at the college, without trying to bend their relationship in the direction she herself was seeking. I want her, she thought. I don't necessarily have to have her right now. I can wait. I'm patient. But I want to nudge it that way. I guess I want her to know, before I take her home, that I want her, and that I'm willing to take it as slowly as she wants to.

"Have you ever been married?" Arthell asked her at one point.

Laura shook her head. "Never."

"I've got this guy who wants to marry me." Arthell sighed in such a way as to indicate that he was a gigantic pain, which made Laura's heart flutter excitedly.

"I take it you don't want to."

Arthell made a sour face and shook her head. "It's nice to be asked, though. I have two friends who got married because they were sure no one else would ever ask them." She smiled enchantingly at Laura, the smile that made Laura's blood shriek happily and started prickly little beads of moisture oozing deep inside her pussy. "I'm glad you're not because it gives me courage to stand up for what I want and not just give in to what everybody else is doing."

There's a reason why I'm not, Laura wanted to say. But she quickly thought better of it. "Can I get you another glass?" she asked, noticing that Arthell was down to the ice cubes.

"I better not have another," Arthell laughed softly. "I'll have to pee before I get home. What if there's a traffic jam on the bridge?"

"I have an idea," Laura said, getting up and retrieving Arthell's nearly empty glass, taking it with her own and heading for the kitchen. "Why don't we just hang out and go to dinner here in the city and drive back later after the rush hour traffic has thinned out a bit?"

Oh god, please say yes! I can't think of any way to move this forward, and I need a little more time with you!

But Arthell shook her head. Laura's heart sank, and it was all she could do not to let her face sink too.

"I have a study group tonight. I really need to be there. They sort of depend on me, if you know what I mean."

Laura's shoulders sagged, but she took a deep breath. "Maybe next time."

Arthell had followed her into the kitchen while talking. Feeling her close behind, Laura turned suddenly and with her elbow knocked over one of the iced tea glasses, which fell to the tile floor and shattered at their feet. Cold ice cubes and water splashed their ankles.

"Oh shit!" Laura gasped. "God, how could I do that!"

Arthell, looking down, backed up a little. She bent down at picked up a couple of the larger shards of glass as well as an ice cube. "Where do you want me to put these? Is there a trash can around here somewhere?"

"Under the sink," Laura said, trying to figure out what to do next. "Just step back. I'll get a broom and a mop."

Arthell leaned around Laura, not wanting to step in the mess, but also reaching for the cupboard knob on the door to the trash can. Her breasts brushed Laura's leg. Laura reached behind to open the cupboard door for her, and their fingers met on the knob. Laura pulled the door open, and Arthell deposited the shards of glass in the can. She still held a half-melted ice cube in her palm and looked up at Laura, their faces only inches apart now.

"Don't want me to put this in there," she said. "It'll melt."

"Put it in the sink. Here."

Laura took the ice cube from Arthell's palm, which was still wet. But her eyes never left Arthell's face. This lovely girl. Her smooth dark brown cheek. She smells so good. I've got to kiss her. Oh god, Arthell, please understand. Don't push me away.

This was a moment of suspended animation. It was like a slow-motion scene in a movie, each movement painfully arrested and agonizingly delayed. Arthell's eyes did not leave Laura's either. Laura moved her face closer, closer, letting her eyes drop to Arthell's thick, sensual lips, glimpsing Arthell's pink wet tongue behind her gleaming white teeth. In another split second her own lips were brushing Arthell's, then pushing into them, curving sideways to make their two mouths fit together better, and she was trying to pour all of her throbbing emotion and desire into this one sweet kiss, not knowing if she would ever have the chance to do it again.

Arthell did not try to stop Laura immediately, but neither did she kiss back. After a few seconds, she pulled away.

"That was nice," she smiled politely. "But I'm not that way…"

If you enjoyed this sample then look for **Laura and Arthell Compilation.**

Also by this Author:

Deep Excavation

Chocolate Sandwich

Post-Game Specials

A Breach in the Preacher's Daughter

Deeply Detoured

The Rich Bitch Itch

"Hard" Competition

Little Rich Girls Go First

Superior Playmate

Spicing Up a Business Conference

Green Minds Lead to Colorful Results

Dirty Acquaintance

Menage a Trois

Provisional Test

Holiday Treat and Heat

Sex on the 46th Floor

Sneak, Peek and Squeak

Distance Leads to a Sexual Marathon

Confessions and Steamy Clinches

Screams of Pleasure

Caught in the Act

Pull My Hair and Make Me Come!

The Emperor Wants Your Pussy!

Three on a Bed

No One Can Replace You

Lock Up the Dogs!

Not While She's Looking

Blindfold Me and Lick Me All Over

Do Me Up the Ass Please

Ride 'Em Cowgirl

I'm Going to Come So Fast

Gina Loves the Dick

Bathtub Sex With Frankie

Spanking Gina's Beautiful Black Ass

Finding Marni's G-Spot

Naked and Horny in the Woods

Marni Wants It Hard, Ashley Wants It Wet

Water My Ficus

About the Author

Miranda Mars lives with her cats and her exercise machines with her "special" friend in a suburb in San Francisco. Here is where she lavishly spends scribbling erotica for your, and her own, amusement.

She is especially attracted to dark-skinned women, and uses them as the lovers of the main characters in the stories she writes. She says they're just so hot! So dark-skinned women, BEWARE! :-)

Her stories are also surprisingly VERY ENTERTAINING for MEN!

From the Author

If you'd like to give me comments or suggestions to any of my books, feel free to shoot me an email at:
miranda_mars@awesomeauthors.org.

Check my page on Amazon and my blog for Updates and interesting info.

Author Central - http://amzn.to/14wSFHW
Author Blog - http://miranda-mars.awesomeauthors.org/

If you enjoyed any of my books then please share the love and click like on my books in Amazon.

If you write me a review and send me an email I will send you a free book, or many.
(Just know that these emails are filtered by my publisher.)

Good news is always welcome.

One Last Thing, For Kindle Readers...

When you turn the page, Kindle will give you the opportunity to rate this book and share your thoughts on Facebook and Twitter. If you enjoyed my writings, would you please take a few seconds to let your friends know about it? Because... when they enjoy they will be grateful to you and so will I.

Thank You!

Miranda Mars
Miranda_mars@awesomeauthors.org

www.ingramcontent.com/pod-product-compliance
Lightning Source LLC
Chambersburg PA
CBHW060747180626
46818CB00002B/487